DRAG THING

BOOKS BY VICTOR J. BANIS

FOR BORGO PRESS / WILDSIDE PRESS:

THE ASTRAL: TILL THE DAY I DIE
AVALON
CHARMS, SPELLS, AND CURSES FOR THE MILLIONS
COLOR HIM GAY
DARKWATER
THE DEVIL'S DANCE
DRAG THING; OR, THE STRANGE CASE OF JACKLE
    AND HYDE
THE EARTH AND ALL IT HOLDS
THE GAY DOGS
THE GAY HAUNT
THE GLASS HOUSE
THE GLASS PAINTING
GOODBYE, MY LOVER
THE GREEK BOY
KENNY'S BACK
LIFE & OTHER PASSING MOMENTS: A COLLECTION
    OF SHORT WRITINGS
THE LION'S GATE
MOON GARDEN
THE POT THICKENS: RECIPES FROM THE KITCHENS
    OF WRITERS AND READERS (editor)
SAN ANTONE
THE SECOND TIJUANA BIBLE READER (editor)
SPINE INTACT, SOME CREASES; REMEMBRANCES OF
    A PAPERBACK WRITER
STRANGER AT THE DOOR
THIS SPLENDID EARTH
THE TIJUANA BIBLE READER (editor)
A WESTWARD LOVE
THE WOLVES OF CRAYWOOD
THE WHY NOT

DRAG THING

or

The Strange Case of Jackle and Hyde

by

Victor J. Banis

The Borgo Press
An Imprint of Wildside Press

MMVII

FIRST EDITION

CONTENTS

DRAG THING, BY VICTOR J. BANIS

Special thanks to Lee Appel,
Who had the idea first

ABOUT THE AUTHOR

Writing as V. J. Banis, Jan Alexander, and a host of other bylines, **Victor J. Banis** is the critically acclaimed author ("...the master's touch in storytelling," *Publishers Weekly*) of more than 150 published novels (*Longhorns*, Carroll & Graf, 2007) and nonfiction works, and his short pieces have appeared in numerous journals (*Blithe House Quarterly*) and anthologies (*Paws and Reflect*, Alyson, 2006; and *Charmed Lives*, Lethe Press, 2006). Many of his books are being published by the Borgo Press imprint of Wildside Press. A native of Ohio and longtime Californian, he lives and writes now in West Virginia's beautiful Blue Ridge.

CHAPTER ONE

Poor Dick lasted exactly 48.3 seconds. In less than a minute, he had gone from a robust, feisty, a notably horny, tomcat to a shredded mass of black fur and guts and blood splattered across the walls of the cage. His *Ee-Yow* of surprise and terror had been mercifully brief. In its wake, the scent of fresh blood and suddenly released feces mingled with the chemical odors of the laboratory, creating a pungent perfume.

That did not mean that She Cat Number One, into whose cage he had so recently and hopefully been introduced, was actually through with her would be paramour. She spent the next several minutes reducing the smelly pieces of fur and bone and entrails to smaller and still smaller pieces, muttering angrily under her breath the entire time, a steady stream of *hiss, growl, hiss growl, hiss....*

For their purposes, however, the two white-coated women watching from outside the cage considered the incident over. Doctor Melissa Hyde switched off her stopwatch and washed some errant droplets of red from her hand before she sat at the computer and typed a few brief notes into a file labeled "Alley Thing."

"I think we can conclude that batch was way too potent," she said with a sigh. "Poor guy. He hardly knew what hit him."

"Personally, I would be tempted to go with it just as it is," Janet Jackle said. "Think how many rapists and mashers we could be rid of in no time if we turned the women of the world on to this stuff." She patted the wire of the cage. "Nice She Cat," she crooned. "Good puss." She Cat snarled over her shoulder and continued her efforts to remove every trace of her late would be Romeo.

"The whole point of the project, my dearest," Melissa said, "Is to empower women, not to make monsters of them."

"She Cat is certainly a monster, that's for sure." Janet chortled. From her cage, She Cat hissed in agreement. "Look, so what if we did make monsters of a few women? We would just be balancing the scales a little, if you ask me. God knows there are plenty of male monsters roaming around out there, aren't there, too often using their brute strength to take advantage of women."

"Yes, that is certainly true," Melissa said, "And if we can make women physically stronger than men, and boost their aggressiveness at the same time, we can put a stop to that forever, and that is a goal devoutly to be desired. But my darling, the whole idea of Alley Thing is to liberate women from the prison of male physical dominance. We would do the women of the world no favors if we landed them in cages of a different sort. We do not want women emulating She Cat: ripping their would-be lovers to shreds and going to prison for it."

Janet, who personally thought that there were plenty of men out there who deserved to be ripped to shreds—she could think of one or two she wouldn't mind tearing into herself—shrugged.

"Well, we know we're on the right track, anyway," she said matter-of-factly, "It's just a question of fine-tuning the formula. Do we feed She Cat before we go?" She slipped out of her white smock.

"I think she's taken care of that for herself." Melissa thought for a moment and made another brief note in her file and closed it. "That was the last of our male subjects, wasn't it? We'll need to find some more volunteers."

"Fortunately for us, there's never a shortage of fellas looking for a little action," Janet said. "What number was this last one?"

"Number twelve."

Janet wrote the number on a pair of labels and glued them to the vial and the syringe. "That's the end of the B trials. We will have to start with the C series tomorrow." She glanced at her partner and saw her look of dejection.

"Cheer up," she said, dropping an affectionate arm about Melissa's slumped shoulders. "We'll get it. You will, anyway. I know you will. There's no one brighter than you are. And just think of what we're working toward. When we're done, when we've made a success of Alley Thing, no man will ever again dare try to force himself upon a woman. It will change the course of history."

"That certainly sounds wonderful," Melissa said. She glanced at the big clock on the wall and grimaced. "But, you know, darling, we have been working for thirteen hours straight. I think tonight I will settle for a cold beer and a pastrami sandwich."

"And a soak in a tub," Janet said solicitously. "And a nice rub with some pretty smelling oil, to get you properly relaxed, and who knows what else might happen after that? What do you think, Missy?"

"I think I prefer not to be called Missy, if it's all the same to you," Melissa said, but she softened the remark with a smile.

"It's just a pet name," Janet said.

"Then give it to a pet." Melissa motioned toward the cage. "Give it to She Cat. She can be Missy if you like."

"First rule of the business, never give pet names to lab animals. It personalizes them," Janet said. "Never a good thing to do."

"And a good second rule is, be careful about giving them to girl friends," Melissa said. "Particularly to girlfriends who don't welcome them. My dad used to call me Missy. When I hear that name, it makes me feel like a little girl again, all helpless and insignificant."

"Ah." Janet nodded her head in understanding. "And still waiting for that approval from Daddy that never came, I'd bet."

"You're probably right," Melissa said.

"In that case, Melissa it shall remain. Though I still think Missy is cute. And, to be honest, the thought of you helpless in my power is definitely a turn on." She pulled her partner to her and kissed her warmly.

9

For a fraction of a second only, Melissa hesitated. This woman-on-woman thing was still new to her. Then, any reluctance vanishing, she happily and ardently returned the kiss.

The woman thing was new to her in the physical sense, at least. If she were to be completely honest with herself, however, she had entertained fantasies of women for years, all the while that she had played the role of a straight woman. Oddly, those fantasies had usually featured the centerfold types of beauties, airbrushed and silicone-filled and glossy, and not anyone even remotely like this thin, angular woman with the thick glasses and the unmanageable copper hair who more commonly smelled of formaldehyde and ethyl alcohol than she did of flowery perfume.

It was Janet, though, who had rescued her from an abusive relationship into which she had fallen, who had restored her dignity and her sense of self worth to her, and who had made her feel like a whole person again.

It wasn't just gratitude, either, that made her tighten her embrace fleetingly. It was Janet she loved, loved not only for her body but for her mind as well, loved her courageous spirit and her good sound sense.

I am a lucky person, she thought to herself, *to have someone so dear.*

"I'll get my coat," she said aloud, already thinking of that tub, and the rub with the perfumed oil. And the hint of things to follow. Yes, that would be a wonderful antidote to her frustration with Alley Thing. "Let's lock up." She gave Janet a loving smile.

* * * * * * *

Caleb Wald waited until the women had locked the lab door after themselves and disappeared into the elevator before he cautiously emerged from the office across the hall in which he had concealed himself. He used his passkey to open the locked door and slipped into the laboratory they had just left.

Though he was the owner of Wald-Med Pharmaceuticals and Jackle and Hyde's employer, it was part of his agree-

10

ment with the two scientists that he had to keep his distance from the laboratory and their work. Melissa had insisted on that from the beginning: no interference, no nosing around. She would be the one to decide when she had something to give him. In the meantime, they must be free to pursue their goal without any oversight from him. Thus, the need for his stealth.

That agreement, however, though he had sworn to it, was one that it troubled him not at all to violate, at least clandestinely. He was paying for what they were doing, after all, and in his opinion that entitled him to nose around all he wanted, though he was not about to say that to Melissa. At this stage, he couldn't afford to have her get temperamental. He knew how stubborn she could be if she got her back up.

Nevertheless, he snuck into the lab often when they were absent, to check on their work—though for all his efforts he had yet to learn much about their progress.

As usual, he paused as he came in to admire himself in the mirror along the front wall. It was practically impossible for him to pass any mirror without a moment or two of self-admiration. He knew that he was good looking. Tall, maybe just a little heavier than might be considered ideal. *I really will have to cut back on the carbs,* he thought, but without much conviction.

Still, he always liked what looked back at him from the mirror. His thick mop of wavy black hair was truly beautiful, and he had undeniably sexy eyes. Every woman he had ever been with had told him that. Even his nose, which was admittedly a little large for his face, could almost be described as beakish in fact, had been complimented often.

"It gives your face character," was the opinion most commonly offered. He turned sideways now and rolled his eyes hard to the left, to get a better look at his reflection. Yes, it was assuredly true: his nose gave him a noble profile. *No wonder broads adore me*, he thought with a sense of satisfaction.

Reluctantly—he could spend hours admiring himself, and often had done so—he turned his attention from the mirror to the laboratory reflected in it. Almost the first thing that

11

he saw was a syringe and a vial lying on the counter. He picked them up and glanced at the labels: B12.

At least they were making progress, then. On his last visit, they had just started on the B series. And truth to tell, at this stage, progress was direly needed. His backers were getting increasingly impatient with the delays, and the last thing he wanted was their displeasure.

He removed the cover from her cage to check on She Cat. *Jesus*, he thought, his eyes going wide. The beast had gotten bigger since the last time he had looked, and that had been just a couple of nights ago.

The cat caught sight of him and spat at him furiously. By now, he and She Cat were old acquaintances, and not of the friendliest sort either. As he always did, Caleb took a broom from the nearby storage closet and used the stick to reach through the bars of the cage and poke at the cat. She yowled in anger and swatted at the broomstick, trying to get a grip on it. It was all he could do to hold on to it. Obviously the Cat had gotten stronger too, and smellier: she smelled like burning hair.

He wrinkled his ample nose and pulled the broom out. She Cat hurled herself against the door of the cage with a loud *thunk*, trying to get at her tormentor, and he felt a little nip of fear zigzag up his spine. Was it only his imagination, or had the bars of the cage actually bent when she rammed into them? If that animal ever got out, there was no telling what damage she could do. He was pretty sure, too, that he was one of the things she would want to damage. She eyed him with burning hatred.

Nervous, he put the cover back on her cage, careful to stay out of reach of her straining claws. He returned the broom to the closet, looking around to be sure he hadn't left any signs of his visit, and gave another glance at the vial of serum. He was tempted to take it with him and have it analyzed elsewhere, but the women would be sure to notice that it was missing. They would know he had been here and had violated their agreement and there would assuredly be hell to pay. He had too much riding on this project to want to risk a major clash with them now.

Instead, he left the vial and the syringe on the counter exactly where he had found them, and let himself out of the room, pausing for just one more admiring glance at the mirror.

* * * * * * *

They popped into her mind all of a sudden: the vial and the syringe!

It was not until they were in the car on their way home, an Ella tape scatting into the semi-darkness, that Melissa Hyde remembered them. "We left the vial and the syringe lying on the counter," she said.

"It's all right, don't worry about it. There's nobody there at night. No one's going to be in the lab," Janet said with an unconcerned yawn.

"The janitor will be there, won't he?"

"That pansy?" Janet snorted her disdain. "He can't get his mind off his silly frocks long enough to get into any kind of trouble. Stop fretting, my pet, they will be just fine where they are until morning."

* * * * * * *

"Pansies! That's it!" Peter Warren cried aloud.

"Pansies?" Teri Warren paused in buttoning the blue tunic of her police uniform and gave her husband a puzzled glance.

"Pansies," Peter repeated. He pointed at the drawing board before him. "The ball gown I have been working on. That's what I want. White silk, with red pansies cascading over the bodice and down the skirt."

"I don't know, honey," Teri said in a doubtful voice, "It sounds a little, well, off the wall, don't you think?"

Peter grimaced and tossed his pencil aside. It hit the wastebasket and bounced to the floor. "Well, if I am ever going to make a name for myself as a dress designer, I'm going to have to establish my own style. I'm sure never going to do it by copying what everybody else does." He gave a disconsolate sigh and, getting up from the drawing board,

13

popped a movie into the DVD player—Fantasia, his favorite—and dropped into a chair in front of the television as the movie began to play.

"You sound beat, honey. Shouldn't you be taking a nap?" Teri asked. "You'll be walking in your sleep by the time you get to Wald-Med."

"Oh, it's just cleaning—sweeping floors and dusting. It's not like I couldn't do it in my sleep." He watched her strap on her holster and fit the Smith and Wesson into it. "God, I wish you weren't out there at night with all that violence I hear about on television. I worry about you, you know."

"Ah, it's not as bad as you think, believe me," Teri said. "Most nights it's every bit as boring as your janitorial job, if you want to know the truth. Riding round and round, up and down, back and forth, all over town, and then just occasionally you get to chase down some punk or bust a dealer. It mostly comes down to five minutes of adrenalin and eight hours of boredom."

"If only I had a real job," he said morosely, unconvinced, "You wouldn't have to be out there dealing with the dark forces every night."

She came across the room and knelt by his chair. "You have got something even better, darling, you have got a dream," she said. "And you will make it. I know you will. One day you will be a famous designer, like that guy in the magazine ads, Calvin What's-His-Name."

"Calvin Klein," he said automatically, watching the hippos and the alligators on the television screen, cavorting to The Dance of the Hours. He grinned as a hippo in a pink tutu did a *grand jeté*.

"Right. Or that Don Karen fellow."

"It's Donna. Donna Karen," Peter said. "He's a she."

Grimalkin, their blue point Siamese, padded into the room from the kitchen and rubbed against Teri's leg. She reached down absent-mindedly to stroke the cat's fur.

"Okay, Donna," she said. "The point is, you will be big one day too. I'm sure of it."

Grimalkin offered a meow of agreement.

14

"And when I am, will you be happy then?" Peter asked, looking directly at her and momentarily forgetting his movie. "With a dress designer for a husband? You know what everyone will think."

"Probably the same as what Abner Kravitz next door thinks."

"Exactly."

"Oh, that old bigot, who cares? So he thinks that you're gay? So what? Let him think what he likes, and anybody else, too. We certainly know the truth." She kissed him tenderly. "Besides, you don't think I get the same thing all the time? People see me, a woman in a police uniform, the first thing they think is that I'm a dyke. Half the guys on the force are convinced I'm a lesbian. But, hey, I don't care, I like my job, and I still come home to you every morning, and that's when the pudding gets proved, as the old saying goes."

She kissed him again and stood up. "Okay, boy genius, back to the drawing board. There are bad guys out there, and crime on the streets, waiting for me to set things right." She paused at the door. "But I still think you should take a nap."

* * * * * * *

He should have taken a nap. Peter realized later that night that Teri had been right after all. It was all he could do to keep his eyes open as he mopped the floors and dusted the counters at Wald-Med Pharmaceuticals. First floor, second floor, then the third. Mop the floors, dust the desks and the counters, empty the wastebaskets, clean the toilets, wash the sinks. The same old thing every night, one corridor after another, one more office, never a break in the unvarying routine.

He hated his job: the forbidding silence, the sterile walls, the antiseptic smell. The fluorescent lights glared overbrightly. By this time of night his hands stung from the strong detergents and his clothes were permeated with the smell of TSP and Pledge, which no amount of laundering could ever entirely eradicate. Sometimes it seemed to him like he smelled them in his dreams.

If only...he resorted once again to his favorite day-dream, his great white whale of a future, always looming ahead of him, just out of reach, teasing him. If only he could interest one of the big fashion houses in his design portfolio, he would be out of here in a second. It wasn't that his designs weren't any good, either. He knew they were. He sighed.

Why was life always so hard for someone artistic? He thought that things would be a great deal simpler if he were just a mechanic or a plumber.

Yawn. He used his passkey and let himself wearily into the locked research laboratory and glanced at the clock on the wall. It was barely one o'clock in the morning. *Almost two more hours to go*, he thought dispiritedly and he was nearly finished already. Two hours to kill before he could clock out. Maybe he would find someplace secluded and take that nap after all.

He thought of Teri, and wondered where she was just at that moment. Taking a nap in her cruiser, he hoped, though knowing her, he doubted it. More than once he had contemplated abandoning his dream of becoming a fashion designer and looking for a serious job instead, something that would support the two of them and make it unnecessary for her to remain a policewoman. He wasn't cut out to be a mechanic, and he knew nothing about plumbing, but he could work in a department store, couldn't he or—well, there must be plenty of jobs out there, if you weren't too choosey.

In his heart, though, he knew it would make no difference if he did. Notwithstanding his fears, Teri loved her job as much as he hated this one. On the rare occasions when she had seen some action, chasing a thief down, or breaking up a melee between street punks, she had come home to tell him about it with eyes afire. With her body afire too, all charged up and eager to share her adrenaline rush with him.

Then, at least, as they frantically coupled on the bed, he had nothing to complain about. It was only later that the worrying set in again.

He swiped the mop listlessly across the linoleum floor and took a damp dusting cloth from the pocket of his apron to wipe down the counter. *Ho hum.*

16

He was surprised to see the vial and the syringe on the counter. Nothing was ever left out in here, lest the wrong person stumble upon it. The truth was, he had only the vaguest idea of what those two women scientists did here in the research lab at Wald-Med. Even if he had ever found anything before, he would probably have had no clue what it was. He was not scientifically inclined.

There were such things as industrial spies, however, weren't there? You read about stuff like that in the papers. And there had to be a reason why the laboratory door was always locked. When they had hired him for this job, they had impressed on him the need for security, which had left him with the impression that whatever went on here in the laboratory was top secret.

He debated with himself whether he should leave the vial and the syringe where they were, or try to put them away somewhere? He felt certain his employers would not want anything important just sitting about where anyone could put their hands on it—but he had no idea where to put them.

Creak. Scratch. The noise from behind him made him start. He glanced around guiltily, half expecting to see one of the laboratory scientists glowering accusingly at him—but no, he was still alone in the room, the door firmly closed. He was alone in the entire building, so far as he knew.

He heard it again, the scratching sound. Puzzled, he looked around. There was a row of a dozen wire cages along one wall, all of them covered with fitted sheets. When he had first started on the job, they had told him emphatically to leave the cages alone, and he always had done just that, had never paid any attention to them at all—had ignored them so completely, in fact, that he had nearly forgotten they were even there.

Now, however, he realized that the noises were coming from one of the cages. The noise, and an odd smell, like iodine or...*or like spilled blood.* That thought popped into his head unbidden. He grimaced and, curious, he gingerly lifted the cover from one of the cages, the one nearest to him, and peered into it.

"Well, hello there," he said to the cat staring back at him through the bars. "My, you are a big kitty, aren't you?"

17

The unkempt cat regarded him solemnly from her cage. She was not just big, in fact, she was enormous, nearly the size of a cocker spaniel; spotted orange and white, like a calico, but her hair was shaggy and unkempt.

She was certainly not a pretty animal but she looked docile enough at the moment and he was fond of cats. He reached a tentative hand through the bars to stroke behind one ear, just where Grimalkin liked to be petted. For a second or two the cat allowed his attention. Then, without warning, she yanked her head around and bit down hard on his finger.

"Yipe!" he yelled. He leapt backward so violently that he almost fell. With his other hand, he reached at the counter behind him for balance, and felt a sudden prick, and looked down to discover he had stuck himself with the syringe lying there.

In alarm, he snatched it up and looked at it. "Alley Thing," the label read, and beneath that someone had written, "B12." He checked the vial. Its label read the same.

He thought for a moment and breathed a sigh of relief. That was all right, then, surely. B12, it was just some vitamins. Maybe Alley Thing was the brand name, though it did seem an odd name for a line of vitamins.

Maybe that was what the two women scientists were doing here: developing a line of health aids. Or maybe one of them took B12 for energy. It was supposed to be good for that, wasn't it? And the pair often worked long hours. Sometimes they were still here when he came in to clean, so it made sense that they might very well need a pick-me-up from time to time.

The important thing was, whatever was in the syringe, it was surely nothing he need be concerned about. No doubt that was why it had been left out. Probably it was of no importance whatsoever. If you thought about it, they certainly wouldn't have left it out otherwise.

The hand that the cat had bitten, however, was another matter. There was not much blood to be seen but her teeth were plenty long, and they must have gone pretty deep. And there was something downright unhealthy about her appearance, now that he thought of it.

18

He looked around for something to sterilize the wound with, and spotted a jar of alcohol on a shelf above the sink. Holding his hand over the sink, he poured alcohol onto the bite wound. *Yow!* He gave his hand a brisk shake. The alcohol stung, but heaven alone knew what that mangy looking cat might give him. Better a little alcohol burn than an infection.

He glanced again at the puncture wound the syringe had made. For such a tiny wound it looked awfully red already, and it was even swollen a little. For good measure, he poured some alcohol on that one as well. There was no sense in taking chances.

The cat gave a low mutter, as if she were warning him of something. "I hope you didn't do me any damage, you devil," Peter said. He flicked the cover back down over her cage, uncomfortable with her malevolent scrutiny. This time he took special care to stay out of reach of her nasty claws. She threw herself violently against the door as the cover descended over the cage, making the cage rock precariously.

"Golly, you are a vicious beast, aren't you?" he said. "I hope this cage is well secured."

Alley Thing. His thoughts went back to the syringe and he glanced at it again. *That really is an odd name. Thing....*

It was his last thought before he woke up in his own bed hours later.

After the Moes.

CHAPTER TWO

It was 3:00 A.M. in the hood, and the Moes were in their domain.

In the wee hours like this, you could almost smell the fog and taste the sea tang in it. Somewhere in the far distance a mournful foghorn lowed. Hector kicked an empty Pepsi can out of his way, and it rolled into the gutter. *Clackety-clackety-clack*. The racket shattered the stillness of the night. A loose sheet of newspaper sailed by on the wind and draped itself briefly around a telephone pole before billowing on its way.

Hector pulled the hood of his parka up. The pair walking alongside him followed suit. Not that it was cold, it wasn't. It was a warm San Francisco night, late October, when the city got its real summer after the "June gloom" that generally lasted through September. The hoods were more a matter of style than comfort. Gangbangers all wore hoods.

"Getting late," Archie said.

"You got that right," Hector agreed.

"We did good, didn't we?" Tom said.

"For sure," Archie said. "We did real great."

The three Moes honestly considered themselves good guys. Super heroes, sort of, like the guys in the comic books: Batman, for instance, who was their favorite, who prowled the streets at night and sorted things out. Which was kind of what they had been doing, as they saw it: sorting things out.

Of course, they didn't wear Batman's mask and cape, or tights like Spiderman. They were in their usual outfits: black bandanas around their heads—black was their color—and drooping black pants that clung perilously to scrawny hips and looked in danger of falling around their ankles at any

20

moment. The extra large tee shirts they sported hung over their pants and halfway down their thighs and so spared anyone who saw them the glimpses of butt cracks that would otherwise have been revealed by the low-riding pants. Customarily, the gangbanger costume included boxer shorts under the low riders, to cover butt cracks, and the Moes would certainly have worn the prescribed boxers too, if Tom had not been caught trying to shoplift that package of them from Macy's. As it was, he had barely gotten away from the security guards without getting busted, but he had gotten away empty-handed, the result of which was butt cleavage instead of boxers and overly large tee shirts to cover the cleavage—not to mention sparing their half-bare bottoms the chill of the night air.

They did not exactly fight crime, either, not the way Batman did, say, but, like, they did do their share to keep the streets safe from ragheads and slanty-eyes and "Meskins," which, as they saw it, counted as doing good. Never mind that Hector's father was from Tijuana. His mother was white and he had been born in the U.S. of A., so he considered himself totally American, and more than one guy who had suggested he was a beaner had ended up eating his teeth.

Unlike the guy they had left behind in the alley, who had beaner written all over him, whereas the chick had been a total Anglo. Meaning they had felt it their Moe duty to straighten the dude out. As for her, they figured they were doing her a favor by educating her. Plus, they figured they had made her happy whether she liked it or not. Getting porked by the Moes ought to be considered an honor in any chick's book, the way they saw it, even if the chick sometimes didn't appreciate it. They were convinced Batman would have done the same and, hey, what chick wouldn't be proud to be porked by Batman?

Besides, they had let both of them live, hadn't they? Which a lot of gangbangers wouldn't have done, since they might possibly finger you later, but hell, the Moes didn't mind that exactly. It just made their reputation that much tougher, which was how they liked it. When people knew you were badass, it kept them out of your hair.

Yeah, sure, they had broken the guy's knee with a lead pipe, but just the one knee, and that had been to keep him off their case while they took care of his girlfriend. Archie had been all for just tying the guy up, but there was one flaw in that idea, as Hector had pointed out: "We got no rope."

The way Hector explained it, breaking the guy's knee was a lot simpler, and better for him, too. Better than, say, killing him.

As for the bitch, she would have gotten off with nothing but a good time if she hadn't spit in Hector's face. She did it for no good reason, too. All he had said while he was humping her was, "Now, ain't this better than doing it with that pansy boyfriend of yours?" and she had hauled off and thwacked him with a big gob, *splat*, right in his face, so, sure he had busted her jaw. Which was strictly her own fault, anybody could see that. Some people just had no frigging gratitude, that was for sure.

It had totally pissed him off, though, because he had been having a hard time getting his rocks off and had just figured he would go for some head instead, and even he knew she couldn't do that with a busted jaw, so he had ended up whacking off on her belly instead and hoping the guys didn't notice, all of which left him really super pissed.

Still, from their point of view, it had been a successful night. They had taken good care of the chick and they had left both of them alive. They had gotten themselves some strange pussy, plus they had scored some crack out of the dude's pocket, and some cash. All in all, they considered it a good night's work. Batman would be proud of them, they were convinced of it.

"Four, five, six." Hector counted out the money. He palmed the seventh buck for himself and gave the others two bucks each. "Jesus, six bucks is all the cheapskate had on him. What a bummer," he said.

"The guy was a fucking loser," Archie said. It still bothered him a little about busting the guy's knee, but he knew better than to hassle Hector about that. Anyway, Hector was probably right. He usually was. That was why he was the brains of their group. Plus, Hector could be a totally mean dude when he was crossed.

22

"I love this town." Tom said with sudden enthusiasm. He pocketed his two dollars and flashed a big grin at his bros. He had a satisfied ache in his balls and a couple of bucks. It felt good. He felt on top of the world. They were the Moes, and fuck anyone who forgot it.

"You got that right," Archie said.

"Yeah." Hector gave them a baleful look. He could still hear the crunch as the guy's knee had shattered. Personally, he liked the sound. Only, "I should have fucked her again," he said.

The town that the Moes loved was San Francisco. They were only a geographical mile or so away from Union Square and the San Francisco of high-end stores and cable cars and sidewalk cafes, but culturally it was more like a million light years. The stores here were the "nothing-over-a-dollar" variety, cars were where you shopped for a tape deck or some hubcaps, and rats scooted across sidewalks reeking of piss and garbage. All of which was to say, this was their San Francisco. They were, if not the kings, at least the princes of the city. Or at least, of a few streets. For sure, they ruled this couple of blocks in the Mission, anyway.

"What a night." Tom smacked his lips with satisfaction.

"Should have fucked her again," Hector said.

"She sure loved it, didn't she? I'll bet that pansy couldn't even do it," Archie said. He thought for a moment. "I'm still kind of horny, though. Maybe we can find something else to jump."

"Not much out on the street this late," Hector said.

They hadn't seen anybody since they had left the couple back in that alley a few blocks away. The streets were quiet. A lone taxi cruised through a nearby intersection, headlights slicing the night. Somewhere in the distance an F car rattled noisily on its tracks, preternaturally loud in the pre-dawn stillness. Faint snippets of a Beastie Boys number faded in and out on the wisps of fog. The city curled up to sleep for the night.

"You guys smell that dog poop right alongside her?" Tom asked, grinning. "I almost sat in it." He had actually put his hand right in it but he didn't tell them that. Remembering, he brought his hand up to his nose to sniff at it.

Jeez. He could still smell the dog poop. He wiped the hand surreptitiously down the leg of his jeans. *People are such shits,* he thought, disgusted. *There oughta be a law.*

"I thought that was her perfume," Archie said.

"Hyuk, hyuk, hyuk." When he laughed, Tom sounded like he was gagging, in Hector's opinion. Worse, like he was gagging in falsetto, which Hector personally thought was disgusting. *Totally girlie man*, he thought, and said aloud, "I love this town."

"You got that right," Archie said.

They stopped in a doorway to smoke the crack. Archie took it out of his pocket and carefully unwrapped the paper it was in. "What the fuck?" he swore.

"What?" Hector leaned close to look over his shoulder. "What?" he asked again.

"This ain't no crack. It's—it's—"

Hector reached over his shoulder and poked at it with one finger. "Fuck! It's bubble gum," he said.

Archie brought it up to his nose and sniffed. Peppermint. "Shit. Why the fuck would a guy carry chewed up bubble gum around in his pocket?" he asked. Disgusted, he flung the gum into the street.

"I oughta go back there and bust his other knee cap for him, the dumb fuck," Hector said.

"Dudes...," Tom said.

"Plus, I should have fucked her again."

"Dudes," Tom said again. He pointed down the street, to where a woman a block and a half away walked in their direction. Except for hookers, you didn't often see a lone woman on the streets of the Mission and for sure not at this hour of the night. "Check it out."

"Jesus, what *is* that?" Hector asked, squinting.

"Looks like some kind of freak," Archie said.

The Moes stared as she strolled nearer. The woman—if she was a woman—was like no woman they had ever seen before. She was tall, for starters, very tall—at least a foot taller than Archie, maybe even two feet taller, and at six foot two inches he was the tallest of the bunch. Her legs beneath her skirt looked like tree trunks and her arms were massive.

24

Everything about her, in fact, was grotesquely outsized, like some comic book mutant.

Tom was the first to realize what they were seeing: "It's a drag queen," he said, astonished. Drag queens were even rarer on these streets, at this time of night, than real women. A drag queen strolling the Mission in the wee hours was practically begging for trouble.

"No shit. It's the ugliest fucking drag queen in the world," Archie said.

"Jesus, it's that Hulk guy in a dress," Tom said.

"Hulk Hogan?" Archie said, puzzled.

"The green one," Tom explained.

"Oh, I get it," Archie said, nodding sagely. "The Green Hornet dude."

"Sweet," Hector said, grinning. "Dudes, this is gonna be fun. Come on."

He stepped from the doorway and began to saunter up the sidewalk in her direction, the other two trailing in his wake. Still unaware of the Moes, the approaching dragster smiled up at an almost full moon as it drifted in and out of the clouds and hummed tunelessly to herself. She had the look of a woman with nothing more on her mind than an ordinary late-night saunter to enjoy the lovely evening.

She was not, however, an ordinary woman. Not even, Hector thought as they got nearer, an ordinary drag queen. Up close, she appeared even more bizarre than she had at a distance. Her dress, a flowery print wrapped around her sarong fashion, looked as if it had recently hung at someone's window. She wore a fanny pack on one immense hip and on her head a sort of turban fashioned from a towel, the kind found on rollers in restrooms. A makeshift, an adlib kind of drag, then, but the Moes were no specialists in fashion, drag or otherwise. All they knew was that she looked weird, really weird.

They were no more than eight or ten feet from her when she finally looked in their direction and caught sight of them. She stopped in her tracks and peered nearsightedly down her nose at the threesome.

"Good evening, gentlemen," she addressed them. She did not sound worried. Which, Hector thought, was pretty dense of her, considering.

"Hey, you know, we need to talk to you," Hector said.

"Yes?" She smiled politely.

"Well, see, like, we're The Moes, the three of us, you dig, and this is our turf," he said.

She gave him a cautious nod. "I am so pleased to meet you, Mister Moe. And Mister Moe, and Mister Moe," she said, nodding to Archie and Tom in turn, and turned back to Hector. "Now, then, how can I help you, gentlemen?"

Hector gave his crotch a meaningful grab and made smoochey-smoochey noises with his lips. "To tell you the truth," he said, grinning, "we was thinking we could help you, Momma."

Her smile vanished and she planted her ham-sized hands on her hips. "Don't call me Momma, Mister Moe," she said in a firm baritone. "I'm quite sure I am no relation of yours."

Hector was not at all intimidated by her considerable size. It was his opinion that all queers were sissies. Even the gym bunnies with the pumped up arms and the massive chests could be counted on to turn into weeping Jell-O when confronted by a real man and he was sure this freaky looking drag queen would be no different. Besides, he was emboldened to see that while he was chatting with her, his two companions had slunk into positions on either side of her.

The drag queen saw them too, and turned toward Tom. "Go away," she said in an imperious voice. "I command you to vanish."

"Now, Momma, that's no way to talk to a man." Hector took advantage of her distraction to give the vast acreage of her fanny a pat.

Kapow! The next second he was in the air. He flew like a rocket and landed on a nearby garbage can with a bang. A foot-long rat that had been enjoying its supper in the can squealed an indignant protest and darted for an alley.

It happened so suddenly that Hector couldn't quite grasp how he had one minute been patting her fanny and the next he was sitting on the sidewalk in a mess of stinking coffee grounds and banana peels. He shook his head, dazed and temporarily at a loss for breath.

"I said, don't call me Momma!" she said emphatically. "And keep your filthy hands to yourself, creep."

Stunned, Tom and Archie froze in place. In the slow-working machinery of his mind, Tom had just decided that it might be prudent to back away a bit, but he was too laggardly in getting the message to his feet. A hand the size of a catcher's mitt grabbed the front of his jacket and another one started slapping his head from one side to the other. *Whack! Whack! Whack!*

"Ouch! Ouch! Ouch!" he cried.

To his credit, Archie moved as if to come to his friend's aid with one of the karate kicks that had served him well in any number of street brawls, a kick aimed straight for the dragster's crotch.

The kick never reached its target, unfortunately. In something less than the blink of an eye, the drag had let go of Tom's jacket and instead seized Archie's foot in midair. Like Hector before him, Archie found himself suddenly aloft, soaring in an orbit about the head of their would-be prey, while his leg felt as if it were being ripped out of its socket.

"Hey, ow, wait," he squealed, "Let me go, let go."

She did. He sailed through space, emitting a high-pitched series of squeaks and squeals until he landed atop Hector with a loud *Kerplunk*!

Hector gave a howl of agony and cried, "Shit. Get off, me, you fuck." He scrambled to get out from under his sudden burden.

Tom made no pretense of heroics. He was not much of a thinker, but in a situation like this, he thought very clearly that it was every man for himself. He turned and ran without a backward glance.

Archie and Hector, seeing her attention momentarily fixed on Tom's fleeing back, scrambled to their feet and tried to run in the other direction. Hector's left arm hung down limply while Archie dragged one leg and hopped frantically on the other, which made for a slow shuffling process. Hector easily outdistanced him, bad arm and all, and disappeared around the nearest corner, but Archie paused to look back, scared that she might be after them. If she was, he had decided his only hope would be to drop to his knees and plead for mercy. He thought that this was no time for pride. He knew he didn't have a chance of outrunning her with his leg hurting the way it was and, strong as she was, he was certain now that he couldn't outfight her.

He was relieved to see that she was still where she had been, though, hands on hips, looking after them with a big grin on her face.

"Hey," Archie shouted, leaning against a brick wall and trying to ignore the pain in his leg. "Who the hell are you?"

"Me?" For the first time since they had met her, she looked unsure of herself, as if she didn't know the answer to that question either. "I'm—er...." She hesitated, her face screwed up in a thoughtful expression.

"Come on, you gotta have a name," Archie said. "Everybody's got a name, don't they?"

From around the corner, Hector said, "Forget it, man, let's go," but Archie stood—or rather, leaned—his ground.

"I do have a name, of course I do. My name is...." Again she hesitated. Then she threw her head back and gave a loud guffaw. "It's Thing," she said.

"Thing?" Archie said in confusion. *What kind of fucking name was that?*

"My name is Thing," she repeated, sounding altogether pleased with the revelation. "Drag Thing, to be exact." With that she turned and sauntered away, still chortling to herself.

Archie followed Hector around the corner and found him backed into a darkened doorway, his eyes wide.

"Jesus, what happened there?" Archie asked.

"I think we just had a nightmare," Hector said, anger taking over for his fear. "That fag, Tom, did you see him just take off running like that, the chicken shit, I thought we was Moes, we're supposed to help one another out, ain't we? Come on."

Personally, Archie thought Tom had shown rare good judgment in running. In retrospect, he wished he had thought of it sooner himself, while he still had two good legs. But he didn't think it wise to say that to Hector when he was sore. "What are we doing, bro?" he asked instead.

Hector, who felt that his role as captain of the Moes had been compromised by the events that had just occurred, thought it essential now to reestablish his leadership. "Just come on," he said. For the first time in his life instead of dodging cops, he was looking for one to flag down. "And hope and pray we don't run into that Drag Thing again."

* * * * * * *

By the time Drag Thing had gone two blocks, however, she had all but forgotten the Moes in the thrill of her new discovery: a shop called For The Girls. At first glance it might have been taken for just another woman's store, but it took no more than a second glance to see that the clothes and accessories in the window were actually meant for men who wanted to dress as women. For one thing, most of them were huge. Even the wigs in the far corner, cascading down Styrofoam heads, were overlarge.

In her opinion, the dresses were tacky, though. She had an idea that she knew someone who could do much better for her than these, although at the moment she could not quite get that information to come into focus. Someone…she was sure of it. It would come to her in due time. Her memory was oddly fuzzy.

But the wigs, now…her eyes fell on a platinum blonde creation, in a Farrah Fawcett style. Twenty-nine ninety-eight, the tag said. *Cheap*, she thought, *for such a beautiful head of hair.*

"Hair," she said aloud. "That's what I need. Hair. Turbans are so out." She whipped the makeshift turban from her head and tossed it into the street.

Of course the store's entrance door was locked at this time of night, and, for some reason that she did not examine, she felt certain she was not likely to get back to shop in the morning, during normal business hours. She looked around and her glance fell on a broken piece of brick lying in the gutter. She picked it up and hefted it in her hand.

"We oughtn't to be naughty," she said aloud. "We really oughtn't." After only a moment's hesitation, she lobbed the brick through the plate glass window. *Crash!* A shower of glass crystals rained down upon the sidewalk.

An alarm went off inside. *Pooh, now the police will be on their way,* she thought. Well, she consoled herself, her shopping would not take more than a minute, surely. She grabbed the blonde wig and plopped it on her head, unmindful of the fact that it was askew. She found a wallet in her fanny pack and took out a wad of cash, fingering through it. She slapped bills down in the window in quick succession. A five. *Slap.* Two more fives and a ten. *How much was that?* She counted out five ones and tossed them down beside the naked Styrofoam head. *That was thirty, wasn't it?*

She was about to go when she noticed the make-up display. *Yes, of course,* she thought, *I must have makeup too. And perfumes, you had to have perfume to be a real woman.* There were bottles and bottles of perfumes here, and lipsticks. She grabbed a handful of the lipsticks and checked them for color. *Too red. Too orange. Ugh.* It was certainly evident that some people had no sense of style.

Inside the store, the alarm continued to ring ceaselessly. Clearly this was taking far too long. The police would be coming any minute now, wouldn't they?

The police—something about the police teased her mind; but there wasn't time now for her to think about that. She must away. She snatched up a huge purse from the window display and raked the entire array of makeup into it: lipsticks and rouges, mascara and scents, a full arsenal of quasi-feminine pulchritude.

Oh, dear, she thought, looking at the cash she had left. She really did not have time to add up her "purchases" and the money she had didn't look like enough anyway. On the other hand, she truly did not want to cheat anyone either. She was not a dishonest person, after all. She had a great respect for the law. She was sure of it.

She fumbled one of the lipsticks out of the purse and used it to write on the broken glass: "I.O.U. for all these goodies. I promise to come back and pay." She signed it

Drag Thing and as an afterthought added a final, "I truly do promise."

A wail in the distance warned of the approach of a police car. She started to go, and saw an enormous pair of shoes on a platform at the rear of the window, wonderful strapped things with towering heels and all aglitter with sequins that blinked an invitation at her.

How on earth had she missed those? She grabbed them as well before she turned and ran, her long, powerful legs eating up the distance in a flash, so that she had already vanished into the foggy night by the time the police car roared to the curb outside For The Girls.

As she ran, Drag Thing sang under her breath, and unfailingly out of tune, that song about how hard it was to be a woman.

CHAPTER THREE

It was a contradiction, of sorts, but it was at times like these—in the wake of some action on the street—that Teri felt most like a woman.

"It was really something," she told Peter, her voice vibrant with excitement. "These street toughs flagged us down, two of them, they're part of a trio who call themselves The Moes. I've tangled with them before, and usually they take off running when we come around, you know, and here they were tonight, jumping up and down and waving at us. And when I got a look at them, they looked like they had been through a war zone. One of them had to be taken to the emergency room, even. His leg was messed up."

Teri's dark eyes flashed with eagerness as she undressed. Action on the job never failed to turn her on sexually, and this time was no exception. Her fingers fairly flew over the buttons of her uniform. In a moment her tunic was gone, and her bra after it. She tossed them aside impatiently.

"Street toughs," Peter said in a puzzled tone, running his fingers through his rumpled hair. "The Moes, did you say they called themselves? You know, it's funny, but, I had the strangest dream earlier, there were some guys like that in it, too...."

He had awakened only minutes before, sprawled naked across the bed and with the most overwhelming headache he had ever in his life experienced. It felt like all the hangovers of the world rolled into one monstrous one. But, why would he have a hangover? He couldn't remember drinking anything. In actual fact, he rarely drank more than a single beer or a glass of wine, and never on work nights.

"And here's the really crazy part, they hadn't even been in your usual street fight with another gang," Teri said, shedding holster and gun, "They said it was just one drag queen who had worked them over. Can you imagine, one little drag queen beating the crap out of a gang of tough street punks. Well, not so little, I guess. They said she was enormous. Eight feet tall, if you can believe them, which is probably an exaggeration. I mean, they wouldn't want to admit they had been worked over by someone normal sized, would they? And she called herself Drag Thing, they said. Isn't that funny? Usually, you know, they give themselves women's names, Delora or Angelina, something like that."

The name seemed to ring a bell in Peter's mind, but he couldn't quite put his finger on what it was. "Drag Thing? What…what kind of a name is that?" he asked. "It sounds like someone was pulling their legs."

"Someone pulled one leg, that's for sure," she said, "Pulled it right out of a socket. It had to be reset." She dragged her trousers down and kicked them aside. "It was for real, though, that name I mean, because just a little while later we got a call on a break-in a few blocks away, and someone had cleaned out a shop window, For The Girls, it's a specialty shop for drag queens—you know, shoes, makeup, the works—and the perp left a sort of I.O.U. written on the glass in lipstick. Signed it Drag Thing." She rolled down her panties, threw them aside too, and grinned excitedly at him. "Guess what I want to do?"

"Uh, you just got home," Peter said, his head still pounding from his mysterious hangover. "Aren't you hungry, honey? Don't you want to eat something?"

"You bet I do." She grabbed him by the arm and hurried him toward the bed he'd just gotten up from. For the moment, he forgot his headache. Teri could be very persuasive when she was excited.

* * * * * * *

Later, freshly showered and smelling of Chanel Number Five, Teri sniffed the air and followed the scent of bacon frying. She found Peter in the kitchen at the stove fixing her breakfast. He was still naked except for a frilly little apron he had tied on that left his backside enticingly bare.

"What's this?" she asked. She held up a large piece of blue-and-white fabric.

Busy flipping slices of bacon, he said, without turning from the stove, "I don't know; where was it?"

"On your sewing machine." She came and kissed him on the back of the neck and gave one of his naked buns an affectionate pat. He slipped the spatula under an egg to flip it and glanced at the dress in her hands.

"Oh." Something totally weird flashed in his mind when he saw it, and was gone too quickly for him to seize hold of it. "It's...it's a dress," he said.

"Okay, I can see it's a dress, but for whom?" she asked, turning it around in her hands. "Or maybe I should say, for what, an elephant? This thing is huge."

"I, uh, I was thinking of the big girls," he stammered. "You know, the oversized ladies. It's a niche market that isn't very well served right now, it seems to me. It's just something I was playing around with, an experiment, sort of."

"Well, you're the designer." She shrugged and took the dress back to where she had found it at the sewing machine. She could not help being just a little curious about it, though. He had never before mentioned doing dresses for the oversized market. She knew that for his designs he really liked the model-type figure, long and slim, skinny, actually. Even she was too full figured to be the kind of pencil thin fashion model for whom dressed designers generally designed their dresses and who wore them on the runways at the fashion shows. She could not imagine Peter even being interested in designing for big women.

Halloween was only a day or so away, however, and she might have supposed that he had made the dress as a costume for himself, if it were not so obviously too large even for him.

Although they had never discussed it, she knew that he was attracted to women's clothes—designing them, of course, but she suspected there was more to it than merely that. More than once, she had looked in one of her dresser drawers and saw that he had been surreptitiously handling her under things. Once, a pair of her panties in the laundry hamper had what she would have sworn were semen stains. She had never questioned him about them, but she was certain that he secretly longed to "dress up," and one time she had realized that he was wearing some of her Chanel Number Five perfume.

The funny thing was, she had not yet come up with any tactful way to let him know that the idea appealed to her too. The Chanel on him that one time had acted as an aphrodisiac on her. Drag in and of itself did not, probably because in her mind she generally associated it with gay men, even though she did know, from reading those advice columns in the papers, that there were lots of men who were entirely heterosexual but who nonetheless liked to cross dress.

It was not that she had anything against gay men either. She had any number of gay friends, including their downstairs neighbor, Lee, and she truly treasured her friendships with them, but those men did not, however, turn her on sexually.

Peter did, and she knew without a doubt that he was not gay. For one thing, he was the best partner in bed that she had ever known. He seemed to know merely by instinct what to do to make a woman happy, and no one could be homosexual who was turned on the way he was by a woman's body, although she suspected that his actual experience with them was not very vast. She had an idea, in fact, that he might even have been a virgin when they met, though she had not been.

His heterosexuality, however, only made the thought of his dressing up like a woman just that much more of a turn on for her. The idea of picking out dresses for him, of helping him with bras and panties and stockings, even putting on his make up, stirred her sexually. *Maybe after breakfast....*

Unfortunately, though she had made some subtle comments now and again, she had not yet managed to get her message across to him. She could see that it was a sensitive subject for him, one that embarrassed him, even—probably, it was that suggestion of homosexuality attached to it that bothered him—and she wanted to find a way to bring it up that did not make him uncomfortable. A woman could not just say to her husband—especially to a husband that she could see was shy about the subject—"honey, I would love to see you in a dress."

Grimalkin, who was invariably miffed whenever she and Peter had sex, came to her and rubbed jealously against her leg. She picked him up and gave him a quick hug. "Cats are supposed to be psychic, aren't they, Grimmy?" she asked. "Couldn't you hint to him about dressing up for me?"

Grimalkin sniffed and gave her a searching look, as if there were something he thought she ought to know.

"See what you can do, won't you?" She kissed his nose and put him on the floor. With a muted meow, he turned his back on her and marched disdainfully away, tail aloft. *People*, he seemed to say with scorn.

Back in the kitchen, Teri poured herself a cup of coffee and sat at the Formica topped table. Peter come from the stove to set a plate of bacon and eggs, cooked exactly the way she liked them, in front of her.

"Dig in," he said.

"Umm, looks great." She took a bite and added through a mouthful of wheat toast and eggs, "By the way, you look really cute in that little apron, honey."

The apron was not one of those "man-in-the-kitchen" jobs either, but definitely a woman's apron, pink and white and ruffled all over—as close, she supposed, as he had yet gotten to dressing as a woman, and he did indeed look cute to her in it. She chewed her toast and when he turned back to the stove, she looked at his naked derriere and thought seriously about biting into one of his shapely little buns.

"Well, gee, if you say so." He blushed all over, even his buns turning pink, but she could see that the remark had pleased him. He looked over his shoulder and flashed his especially adorable shy grin—the one that started slowly at his mouth and took a moment to reach his eyes—before he turned back to the skillet and his own eggs.

It was a start, she thought. *Today, aprons, tomorrow, fish net stockings*. She began to eat her breakfast with the hearty appetite she always displayed after their sexual episodes.

36

"You know, Bunny," she said—a nickname generally saved for their most intimate moments—"You are the best little hubby any policewoman could wish for."

Grimalkin had followed her into the kitchen. He rubbed impatiently against her bare leg, as if he had something on his mind.

* * * * * * *

It was Grimalkin who later led Peter to the outlandish collection crammed into the laundry hamper. The Siamese sat on the floor and meowed repeatedly at the hamper as if trying to tell him something.

"What's up, buddy?" Peter asked and lifted the lid on the hamper. He gasped at what he discovered there: an enormous length of garish floral patterned drapery, a silver blonde wig, high-heeled shoes covered with sequins, a red purse which, when he hastily opened it, turned out to be stuffed full with make-up—lipsticks, perfumes, rouge, mascara, liner. His head swam as he stared at purse's contents.

That dream he'd had...he flashed back on that. It had been a dream, hadn't it? Surely that could not have been real. But if it was not real, if it was only a dream, then how had these things come to be here, in the hamper? And hadn't he dreamed, too, about filling a purse with make-up? It was all kind of vague, like one of those conversations you only half heard on a bus or in a bar.

"Honey, I'm going to do some laundry before I go," Teri said from the bedroom. Peter snatched the clothes and the purse from the hamper and threw them behind the shower curtain and pulled the curtain closed. The lid of the hamper dropped with a bang, making Grimalkin jump. He swished his tail angrily and stomped out of the bathroom. Things were going very strangely around here, it seemed like to him.

Teri stepped over the disgruntled cat as she came into the bathroom and picked up the hamper. "Funny," she said, giving it a shake, "I would have sworn this was heavier when I picked it up earlier. Oh, well. Might as well get it done anyway."

"Leave it, why don't you. I can do laundry later," he said.

"Oh, I've got plenty of time. You work on your designs."

She took the hamper with her, paused in the kitchen for the detergent and bleach, and blew him a kiss as she let herself out the door.

When she was gone, Peter frantically snatched the things from behind the shower curtain and looked at them with a mounting sense of panic. What was he going to do with all this? He couldn't leave it here, that much was certain. Teri would be sure to find it sooner or later.

He went into the bedroom, dragged a big battered backpack off the closet shelf, and carried it hurriedly back to the bathroom, where he stuffed the wig, the fabric, the shoes, and purse into it. As an after thought, he went back to the living room to fetch the dress that Teri had found earlier on the sewing machine.

He had only given it a glance before. Now he held it up to look carefully at it. It was a beautiful fabric, a sea blue silk with a delicate white floral pattern running through it. He remembered the fabric all right. He had gotten it just a week or so ago, but the last he remembered, it had been neatly folded on his fabric shelf in the closet.

How on earth had it found its way to his sewing machine, and practically finished as a dress? Teri was right, too: it was huge, too big even for the women who constituted the "full figure" market, despite what he had told her. It might have been made with a drag sumo wrestler in mind. A particularly large sumo wrestler at that, he amended.

It was all too much for him to comprehend. He went back to the bathroom with the dress and stuffed it into the backpack with the other things and hid the backpack well behind his clothes in the closet. He would have to take it with him to work and try to find someplace there to hide it. Or, maybe he could just toss it all somewhere—say, in a dumpster between here and there. He was pretty sure there was one behind the Safeway store.

What had happened to him? He thought back over the previous night, but his memories were only a blur. He'd had those bizarre dreams, and had awakened with a splitting headache just before Teri got home.

But wait, now that he went back over them, not all of his memories were so fuzzy. He could remember the early part of the night clearly enough. He remembered arriving at work and feeling sleepy, and bored; nothing unusual about that. And he remembered, too, the laboratory, and—it came back to him in a flash, like a picture on a screen—the vial and the syringe he had found on the counter.

The syringe with the vitamins. Yes, that was it. It was after he had accidentally injected himself with that Alley Thing vitamin B12 that everything had gone blank.

He looked at his hands. The puncture wound from the syringe had vanished altogether. Even the marks where the cat had bitten him had healed up completely. There was no trace left of either of them. Whatever was happening to him, it was not the result of an infection, then, at least not from either of those. Actually, he had never known wounds to heal so completely so quickly. Still, he had to assume that the gap in his memory somehow connected to the syringe with the vitamins.

What if…? The thought sent a shiver up and down his spine…. *What if that hadn't been vitamins in the syringe? What if it was…?* But here his mind balked. What on earth could it have been if not vitamins?

Alley Thing. He puzzled over the name. *What could that mean? As far as that went, what were "alley things?" Rats, of course. And Cats. Homeless people and muggers. How did you put things like that into a syringe? And why?*

Muggers. His mind circled back to that thought. *Street toughs. Like the ones in his dream. Like the ones Teri had mentioned. The Moes, she called them. Could there be a connection? But what, and how?*

One thing he knew for sure: he needed to talk to those women scientists at Wald Med. They were the ones with the answers.

Holy Moley, he thought with mounting dismay. *What have I done to myself?* Something really weird was happening, that much was obvious.

DRAG THING, BY VICTOR J. BANIS

* * * * * * *

He was just too weird, in her opinion. Gladys Kravitz sniffed and averted her eyes when Lee Appel came into the laundry room. It was not that she exactly disapproved of homosexuals, not really. Live and let live, was her motto. After all, she was a medical professional. She had seen it all in her forty-plus years as a registered nurse. People were just people, she liked to say to the other nurses.

On the other hand, male people of *that* persuasion did not have to flaunt themselves, did they? And a man dressing as a woman—which Lee tended to do a lot when he was not working—was definitely flaunting himself, in her opinion.

It especially galled her because he was a nurse too. It might have been different if he were, well, a civilian, so to speak. But, a nurse…She regarded his habit of cross-dressing as a slap at the whole profession and maybe even at all of womanhood as well. If nothing else, it was undignified for a trained medical person.

Worse yet, he didn't even go to the trouble to try to make himself look like a *real* woman—not that he would have fooled anybody, but still the attempt might have evidenced a little sincerity on his part. His beard, full and bushy, just looked bizarre with the housecoats and peignoirs and frilly dresses that he favored when he was off duty. Say what you might about sexual tolerance, and it was no kind of bias on her part, but she felt most certainly that a man with a beard just looked silly the way he was dressed this morning, in a muumuu and mules.

"Good morning," he greeted her cheerily. As always, he seemed to be entirely oblivious to her disapproval. Which only irked her the more. The very least he could do was act repentant.

She sniffed again and nodded without speaking or even looking at him. Thankfully, her laundry was all but done. She folded the last of her husband's boxer shorts, hoping fervently that Mister Appel was not paying undue attention to them—Abner most certainly would not want his most personal items ogled by a man in a muumuu, she felt sure. He might not even want to wear them after they had been contaminated like that, and who could blame him? She gathered up her things and went to leave, and nearly bumped into that Warren woman, the policewoman, coming through the door just at that moment with her own basket of laundry.

* * * * * * *

"That woman is not a happy camper," Teri said, setting her basket on the counter.

"It's my costume," Lee said with a shrug. "Though I can't think why she should object to it. It's such a nice print, really. I like the colors. Green and blue. Sky blue, as a matter of fact. And it's from Macy's, it's not like I got it at Ross or some outlet store." He glanced down at himself. "Maybe it's the green. It is kind of olive-ish, isn't it? Does it make me look sallow, do you think?"

"I think it's lovely," Teri said. "She is probably just jealous. I mean, the woman wears chenille. Puh-leeze."

Lee giggled. "Really. Puh-leeze. And speaking of women's wear, how is our favorite designer?"

Teri began sorting her laundry into piles. "To be honest, I'm not sure," she said thoughtfully. "He seems to have something on his mind. Something troubling him, you know what I mean?"

"You are surely not thinking that he is straying? I mean, men do, of course. They're like a bunch of tomcats, most of them, aren't they? But not our Peter, surely."

Teri did not miss the faintly hopeful note in Lee's voice. She understood perfectly. She knew full well that Lee had a major crush on her husband. Far from disconcerting her, it made her feel sympathetic. She knew just as well that his chances of ever consummating that love were non-existent.

Anyway, how could she blame anyone for adoring her Peter, cutie that he was? She was happy to know that Lee and Peter were good friend—and nothing more. She even allowed herself to hope that someday Lee's penchant for dressing up in women's clothing might wear off on Peter.

More than once, she had thought about enlisting Lee as an ally in her plans to get Peter into a dress, but, really, it was her hope that the idea, when it came, would be Peter's alone—well, with maybe just a little nudge or two from her in that direction, but without outside prompting. When it happened, she wanted it to be utterly intimate, something private to be shared by the two of them alone. With Lee involved, it would be more of a camp thing; funnier, but less sexy, somehow.

"No, nothing like that," she said. "It's just...I don't know. He seems worried about something, but he keeps insisting everything is just fine."

Lee shrugged. "I could stop by later and visit. Maybe it's one of those guy things, you know, that men are embarrassed to talk about with women."

"I don't know...," she said hesitatingly.

"And I am a guy, you might have noticed, despite the muumuu."

"You may be right," Teri said with a sigh. "Would you mind stopping by, just to see if he has anything he wants to say?"

"*No problema.*" Lee was always happy to stop by for a visit with Peter. He knew that his crush on his neighbor was hopeless, but that didn't hinder him from engaging in his fantasies. Anyway, Peter was a nice guy, and he genuinely enjoyed his company. And he did design the most divine frocks. Once, he'd actually made a special gown for Lee, which was his all time favorite. It was so deliciously tacky. You just couldn't find dresses like that in the catalogs.

"How's the writing coming, by the way?" Teri asked.

"Oh, writing." He shrugged. "It's like taking a piss in a windstorm, you know: you put a lot out but when you're done it seems like there is not much to show for it. I'm doing an article on Halloween in the Castro, for the Bay Area Reporter. Yawn."

"It will be fun, I'm sure," Teri assured him. "I always love your pieces."

"Can I help?" Lee asked, indicating the laundry she was sorting. "I'm all finished with mine."

"Oh, no...." Teri hesitated. She had put Peter's jockey shorts and the jockstrap that he wore when he jogged into a separate pile. "Well, you could put those in washer for me while I finish sorting out the rest."

"Gladly," Lee said with genuine enthusiasm in his voice. He scooped up the pile of dirty underwear. Teri discreetly turned her back while he loaded them into a washer. If he were going to do anything kinky, like sniffing them—which she had been known to do a time or two herself, all those raunchy male scents—she thought she would just as soon not see. What she didn't know couldn't hurt her any.

At the washer, Lee paused to take just the quickest, tiniest sniff.

* * * * * * *

"He's wearing a muumuu today," Gladys told her husband when she got back to their apartment.

Abner Kravitz harrumphed his disapproval. "Damned fruits," he said from behind his newspaper. "Maybe it is time we moved. There's too damn many of them around here, if you ask me. Him downstairs, and that fairy dress designer next door, and…."

"Peter Warren? But he's married," she said, opening and closing closets and dresser drawers.

"To a dyke."

"What makes you say that?"

"Come on, a woman cop? Of course she's a dyke. It's one of those marriages of convenience you read about in the papers. Some jobs you got to keep up a front."

Gladys frowned while she put shirts on hangers. She could not think why a dress designer would need to keep up a front. For that matter, in San Francisco, it did not seem to her like a policewoman needed to worry over much about that sort of thing either. Didn't she read that the San Francisco Police Department actively recruited from the gay community?

Besides, that nice Mister Warren next door was so polite. And so cute, too. She just could not imagine anyone that attractive being homosexual, not when he could have his pick of women. Even older women, if he was so minded. The other nurses said that young men often liked older women. And the way he sometimes looked at her, she could not help wondering. Really, she wasn't *that* much older. And she was a nurse, a professional woman…Men liked a woman they could respect.

"She just needs a real man, is all, that's all any of those women need to straighten them out," Abner said. His newspaper rustled as he turned a page. He segued back to his earlier comments. "The problem is, where would we move to in this town? They're all over the place. You can't get away from fags and dykes, everywhere you turn. Like flies on garbage."

"Oh, that reminds me," Gladys said, slamming the last drawer shut. "Don't forget to take out the garbage."

* * * * * * *

Later, when Gladys, dressed in cheery flowered scrubs and sensible nurse-shoes, had gone off to work, Abner remembered the garbage. He tugged the plastic bag from the can and stepped out to take it to the chute at the end of the hall, and there she was, the dyke cop, just getting off the elevator with her laundry.

As he strolled down the hall in her direction, a sock fell out of her basket. She set the basket down on the floor and bent to pick up the sock. Her curvaceous rump made a target too tempting for him to ignore. Abner slid a hand quickly and lightly over it as he passed.

"Whoa!" she exclaimed, straightening and turning towards him. "What's with the hands, Buster?"

"Sorry," he said, smirking and looking not at all apologetic. "I tripped. Kind of lost my balance, you know?"

"*You* know, you can be arrested for sexual assault, Mister Kravitz." She gave him her cop-glower.

"Look, it was an accident, okay, don't get your drawers in a knot," he said sharply. He went past her toward the garbage chute.

"Well, you want to be a little more careful," she told his back. "People can get hurt in accidents. Real bad."

"Yeah, I'll watch myself," he said without looking back. Like, he was worried about a dyke cop. What was she going to do anyway: tell her fag husband? Who'd probably come over and beat him with a powder puff.

44

He laughed aloud to himself at that idea. A powder puff. Might be kind of fun, if you thought about it. "Here, hit me here, please, Mister Fag, oh, again, please." He laughed again.

* * * * * * *

Peter was furious when she told him about the incident. "That creep," he said angrily. "I ought to go over there and punch him in the nose. Teach him a lesson."

"Don't you dare," she said. "You'd just get yourself arrested for assault and I would have to come bail you out."

"Maybe. But it would be worth it."

"Forget it. *He*'s not worth it. Besides, you know what he thinks. Dyke and fairy. There's no cleaning up minds like his. The best thing to do is just to ignore them."

"I guess you're right, but it does tick me off. One of these days," he said. He picked up his backpack from the floor by the door.

"What's that?" she asked.

"Oh, just stuff," he said. "Some shirts I'm going to drop off at the Salvation Army box on my way to work."

"That's a bit out of your way, isn't it? Here, I'll drop them off." She reached a hand toward the backpack.

"No, that's okay," he said quickly. He gave her a hurried kiss and was out the door before she could argue.

He practically ran to the elevator. He just hoped those women scientists were still at the lab when he got there.

CHAPTER FOUR

"She's gained two more pounds," Melissa said with a grimace. "Almost a full pound just since yesterday. That's eleven pounds altogether since we started, with no change in her diet. She's ballooning."

She lifted She Cat from the scales and carried the hissing, clawing feline back to her cage. She had barely gotten the door shut before She Cat charged at it, making the entire cage shake violently.

With a weary sigh, Melissa peeled off the wire-enforced gloves and the welder's mask and the industrial apron—all the protective gear that She Cat's nasty temper required. She replaced the cover on the cage and unbuttoned her white smock. "Why don't we make an early night of it, okay?" she said. "How's the blood work looking?"

"It's not good," Janet said, her expression worried. "The serum levels are up by nearly seven and a half percent."

"They should be dropping, not increasing," Melissa said. There was a note of growing concern in her voice. She took off her smock and hung it on a peg on the wall and took her coat off another. "She should be excreting the injections, actually, but she's not. They are all staying in her."

Janet helped her with her coat. "It isn't just staying in her, Melissa. It's increasing," she said. "The injections alone do not account for that much of an increase. Which means that her body has somehow begun producing it on its own."

They exchanged anxious glances. Janet was the first to look away. "She's getting bigger every day," she said. "Look at her: she's the size of a small cougar already. That cat could probably bring down a grown man. And she's not just getting bigger, she's getting nastier, too, every day more aggressive. Melissa, we have to face facts. She Cat is mutating."

After a worried moment, Melissa said, "Yes. But into what?" She glanced at the cage. As if on cue, She Cat gave a vicious yowl and attacked the door of the cage again, making it rock perilously on the edge of its table.

We'll have to get a bigger cage, Melissa thought. *And soon. A much stronger cage. That one isn't going to hold her for much longer.*

"Aggressive indeed," she said aloud. "Janet, have we created a Franken-pussy?"

* * * * * * *

In the elevator, the lab carefully locked behind them, everything properly put away this time, Janet pushed the button for the basement garage. To her surprise, Melissa pushed the one for the lobby level.

"Aren't you coming home?" Janet asked.

Melissa avoided her gaze. "I meant to tell you, honey. I have to meet Caleb."

"Caleb?" Janet was incredulous. "What does that bastard want now?"

"He said he had to meet with me. He said it was urgent. And he is the owner of Wald-Med Pharmaceuticals, after all, the one paying for our experiments. And our boss, need I remind you."

"He is also your ex boyfriend," Janet said. Her voice dripped venom. "Your married ex boyfriend. The one who used to slap you around for kicks, in case you have forgotten that. Why would you want to meet him? You aren't getting any ideas about getting back with that SOB, I hope."

"Absolutely not. I promised you when we started…well, when you and I got together, I promised you that was all over for me. And it is, I mean it. He swore this was strictly business, though. He said he only wanted to talk about something important related to the Alley Thing project."

"Of which I am co-developer, may I remind you? I am coming with you," Janet said.

"No." Melissa said quickly, firmly. "He was very specific. He said, 'me alone'." More gently, she added, "Don't
worry, darling. I'll be all right, really. I insisted on some
place public, so I would not have to be alone with him. He is
a bastard, but he's not a complete fool. He wouldn't try anything funny in public. If he did, and it got in the papers, his
wife would hear about it, and he would be out of a job, just
like that. She's the one with the bucks, and she gave him an
ultimatum when she found out about him and me. Believe
me, he won't want to do anything that would further jeopardize his meal ticket."

"If she'd been smart, she'd have given him the old
heave-ho then and there," Janet said. The elevator slowed to
a stop and the doors opened onto the empty lobby. "And
where exactly is this urgent one-on-one meeting going to
happen?"

"At the Copa Club. On Hayes."

Janet snorted her disdain "That dump?" she said. "You
are not walking there, not at night. I will drive you." When
Melissa looked doubtful, she said, "No ifs, ands, or buts; I
will drive you." She pushed the elevator button. The doors
closed again with a whoosh.

Melissa had a glimpse of their janitor, Peter Warren,
hurrying through the lobby doors, looking very worried
about something. He waved when he saw them. Melissa
waved back as the elevator doors closed.

*　*　*　*　*　*　*

Peter had just the briefest glimpse of the two scientists
as the elevator door closed. He was too late. Despite the fact
that he had rushed to work and come in earlier than usual,
practically jogged the whole way, the women were already
gone. He stood watching the indicator as the elevator
dropped to the garages, trying to think what he should do.

Maybe he could catch them the garage, he thought; but
by the time that possibility occurred to him, the slow moving
elevator was already on its way back up. They would surely
have driven off before he could even get to the lower level.

He went morosely upstairs instead, let himself into the lab and looked about, but he had no idea what he hoped to find. They certainly were not likely to make the mistake of leaving something out a second time, and of course he was right. The empty counters seemed to mock his frustration.

And anyway, what if they had left the syringe and the vial out on the counter again, he asked himself, what good would that have done him? He had no idea what they might have contained, if not vitamins. It was the two women he needed to talk to, to demand explanations from, and he had missed them.

A noise from the row of cages reminded him of the nasty cat who had bitten him the night before.

Cat. The word popped into his mind. *Alley Thing,* he thought, and then, a second later, *Alley cat.* Was the cat somehow the key to it all? It seemed preposterous. How could a cat's bite have caused what had happened to him—if it really had happened, and wasn't just a bad dream? And yet…cautiously, he approached the cage where he had seen the cat the night before and gingerly lifted the cover from it. He didn't want any more cat bites.

He gasped at the sight of her. Even with his naked eyes he could see that the cat was larger than she had been just one night ago. Larger and wilder-looking in some way he could not quite define. She looked truly savage, and certainly dangerous.

The moment she saw him, the cat ran at the door of the cage as if to prove how dangerous she was, but midway there she came to an abrupt halt. She crouched down instead and regarded him with unblinking topaz eyes. The look she gave him was one of pure evil, but of something more as well, something he sensed without really understanding it. The cat almost seemed to be sizing him up in some new, some unexpected way.

He glanced past her. There was something else in the cage with her, littering the floor: bits of hair too dark to be hers and—it almost looked like pieces of a dead animal. Something she had been eating, apparently. A small bit of raw meat clung to her whiskers. His dinner rose in his throat threateningly.

49

They locked eyes and he felt an odd sense of some communication between them, something she almost seemed to be trying to tell him, something he could not put it into words. Not kinship, exactly, but it seemed like a recognition of some sort. The look she gave him now was more speculative than threatening. He could not take his eyes from hers.

After a spellbound moment, he seemed to be falling into their eerie yellow depths.

* * * * * * *

The neon sign outside the Copa Club—a giant cocktail glass with an olive on a spear—flashed yellow and green, green and yellow in the murk of the fog.

Janet pulled up to the curb in front of the club and said, "I'll wait for you."

"No, don't, please," Melissa said, opening the car door. "You go on home and I'll call a taxi when I'm finished. It won't be long, I promise."

For a moment Janet was about to argue but she thought better of it. She knew the look Melissa got when she had set her mind on something.

"Okay, then," she said, "But forget about a taxi. You call me on your cell when you are finished with whatever it is that son of a bitch wants. And I warn you, if you do not call in an hour, I will come looking for you, and if that creep has laid a hand on you, he will not live to laugh about it."

"Have no fears," Melissa said with a grateful smile, and got out. She waited by the curb until Janet had driven away. Watching the Mustang's taillights disappear, she thought of Caleb Wald, waiting inside, and immediately flashed back on that remark Janet had made the night before, about her longing for her father's approval, the approval that had never come.

It was true. Janet had hit the nail squarely on the head: that had always been the great void in her life. Her mother had died when she was little more than a baby, so it had been just her and her father as she was growing up. He had not been a bad man, either. In all fairness, she supposed he had

50

done as good a job as he was capable of in raising her. If anything, she was the one at fault.

At least, that was how she had seen it when she was a child. She just never seemed to quite satisfy his expectations. She so needed to know that he loved her in full and what she got instead had always been a partial payment. He told her often that she was "doing better," and she was "getting there," she was "going to make him proud some day."

Unfortunately, that day had never come. He died of a sudden stroke five years ago, and the unconditional, the all-embracing approval that she had longed for, went to the grave with him.

The emptiness that had left in her had made her vulnerable to other men, particularly to an older, manipulative man like Caleb Wald. She could see now that Caleb even looked a lot like her father, and he too had instinctively recognized her pressing desire for approval and used that as a means of controlling her.

"I just want everything to be perfect with us, Melissa." How many times had he said that to her?

"What I ask is not so difficult, is it?" She had heard that over and over again as well.

"A man expects the woman who loves him, who *says* she loves him, to try to please him. That's only normal."

"It seems to me as if you go out of your way at times to make me unhappy."

She had heard those lines, and dozens more like them, hundreds of times in the months they had been seeing one another. And, always, they had spurred her to work harder and harder to please him, to earn his approval.

In the end, it was Janet who had made her see that what she had thought was her love for Caleb was nothing more than need, the need that had been left unsatisfied in her relationship with her father. And what she had fooled herself into believing was his love for her was nothing more than control. Abusive control. And it was Janet who had helped her to summon the courage to end that control, and the relationship.

To be fair, there was one area, at least, in which she had to give Caleb the credit he was due: though as the head of

Wald-Med he was her boss and Janet's, he had never interfered in their work, had never even come to the laboratory. That had been one of the chief conditions she had put upon their working arrangement, and he had always abided by it. This would be the first time, in fact, that she had seen him since the breakup of their romance two months ago. For a moment, standing on the sidewalk, she felt a twinge of anxiety. From inside the bar, Tammy Wynette faintly urged every woman to stand by her man.

Did I fail Caleb Melissa asked herself, listening to the words of the song? *Should I have stood by him?* The thoughts, guilt laden, came into her head uninvited.

"I just want everything to be perfect with us," he had insisted time and time again. It had not been, of course, and the implication had always been that it was she who had fallen short. Was it true?

"If only you would try a little harder." His voice, like sweet thick cream, taunted her. Then he would smile that smile, the one that told her better than words ever could how very much he did want things to be perfect for them.

If only she had tried a little harder. If only....

She tossed her head angrily derailing that train of thought. No, she would not fall into that trap again. Those honeyed words, that bewitching smile, were no more real, no more wholehearted, than her father's had been, and ultimately no more fulfilling.

She had someone now who truly did approve of her, who loved her without reservation, just the way she was. She gave thanks again that Janet had come into her life to reveal the truth to her. She squared her shoulders and marched through the yellow and green glow of the fog, toward the entrance to The Copa Club.

Janet was right about one other thing, she thought with a grim smile, giving the door a forceful shove: *this place is a dump.*

* * * * * * *

Even Caleb Wald would have admitted that The Copa Club was a dump. Despite the city's no smoking laws, the air smelled of cigarette smoke, blended with the odor of stale beer and too many bodies bathed too seldom.

The bar's chief virtue—really, it's only virtue apart from its proximity to Wald Med Pharmaceuticals—was that it had been one of the places where he and Melissa had safely met in the past, a place where he was not in the least likely to run into his wife or any of her uptown friends.

He was still smarting from the fact that Melissa had broken off their affair. Not that it had not long since grown stale for him, too. In his opinion, which he considered an expert one, she had always been something of a cold fish. At the time, that had really puzzled him, since he knew that he was gorgeous to look at as well as spectacular in the sack. Women invariably adored him. They just could not help themselves. Who could?

Of course, now he understood why Melissa had been so cold with him. He had simply been too much of a man for the lesbian in her.

Still, he always liked to be the one who ended those things. Worse, in this case it had not even really been Melissa who had broken it off, it was that dyke girlfriend of hers, sticking her nose in where it did not belong. Janet Jackle had even done the unthinkable and called his wife, Alice, to tell her what was going on. It had caused him no end of hell.

He would have liked to kill the bitch. Would have liked, at the very least, to toss her from her job at Wald-Med but, to his surprise, Melissa had been absolutely firm on that score.

"If Janet goes, I go," she had said resolutely, and no amount of arguing had been able to budge her from that threat.

As much as he would like to have given Janet Jackle the old heave-ho, he could not afford for Melissa to go with her. He had far too much riding on their Alley Thing project. Ultimately it was going to make a rich man of him, he was sure of it. Rich enough that he could tell Alice where she could stuff her precious money. He would be glad to be done with her, too. It was her money that had attracted him in the first place, and it was only her money that kept him married to her. He was counting on Alley Thing to change all that.

And, like it or not, Alley Thing was Melissa. There was
no question that she was brilliant. It was her mind that had
initially brought them together. When she had first submitted
her proposal for the project, he had seen its potential at once,
and had snapped it up, and her with it, before he even
thought about how beautiful she was.

He was sharp; he knew that. He was clever at making
things happen. With his wife's money and his smarts, he had
parlayed Wald-Med into a company that would soon contend
with the biggest of the pharmaceutical giants. Particularly if
Alley Thing was the success he envisioned.

A lot of his success up to this point had come from
phony government grants. If you knew how to present the
proposal, you could get government money for almost any
study. Take his male hormone pill, for example, marketed by
a subsidiary company that it would be nearly impossible to
trace back to him and sold over the counter for a fraction of
the cost of Viagra. The results of the governmental study,
conducted at one of his own labs, which also could not easily
be linked to him, had been inconclusive.

Of course the results of the study were inconclusive; the
pill was nothing but a clever hoax, but all the media attention
had turned it into an overnight best seller. Stores couldn't
keep it in stock, and even with production cranked up to the
max, he could sell every pill he could produce and then
some. The real bottom line was, you just had to know how to
milk the system, and he was good at that. He was better than
good. He was brilliant.

It was not only business, either. He was just as good,
too, at handling people. He was especially good at handling
women, and bending them to his will.

He was just smart enough, however, to know that he was
not in Melissa's league when it came to brainpower. Her in-
telligence was something he admired at the same time he envied and resented it. In some vague way he could not quite
articulate, it threatened him, which was why he had found it
necessary to sometimes bring her down a peg or two.

Women sometimes needed a bit of slapping around, he
was convinced of it. They weren't really happy without it.
Especially a woman like Melissa. So many times it had

seemed to him that she was lording it over him, showing off her brilliant mind to make him feel dumb. It never failed to infuriate him. Even now, as he thought about her, his fists, resting on the table, clenched and unclenched of their own accord. How he would dearly love to have another whack at her.

There was a quick gust of cold air as the street door swung open and Melissa stepped inside, a wisp of fog following her in. He was relieved to see that she had come alone, as he had insisted. He had half expected the bull dyke to come with her regardless of his instructions. Melissa could be bull-headed.

Heads turned toward her. Even the din of the bar—the too-many-voices-talking-too-loudly, the clink of glass on glass, the wail of the jukebox, the clack and thump from the pool table—seemed to dim as she paused in the doorway.

She was a looker, no doubt of that: petite, with soft brown hair almost to her shoulders and the kind of slim waisted, full busted figure they put on pin-up calendars or centerfolds.

Not a little pleased by the attention she received from the men in the room, which he thought reflected well on him, Caleb got up from his table and hurried across the bar to meet her. He threw a quick glance at the three men who sat at the corner table. They nodded that they had gotten his message.

When he tried to kiss her, however, Melissa turned her head so that his kiss landed on her cheek instead of her lips. He seethed inwardly. The intended kiss wasn't just a matter of showing off for the benefit of the bar patrons, though he did enjoy letting other men see how successful he was with women. He would have liked the three dark-suited men to get a better impression of his ongoing relationship with her. The putzes had really been riding his ass lately. One of these days he would straighten them out.

He would straighten her out as well, as he had sometimes had to do in the past. She might put up a brave front, especially when her lezzy friend was around, but he knew how to deal with difficult women. They just needed a strong hand, applied in the right places.

For the moment, though, he needed her cooperation with the project, and he needed the putzes for their money. *Patience*, he cautioned himself. With women and with business, timing was everything.

He took her arm and steered her to a table, and seated her in view of the men in the dark suits, but with her back carefully turned toward them, so they wouldn't be able to see any reaction on her part. Just in case. Melissa could be difficult, especially now that she had linked up with that restroom groupie. He didn't want them getting the wrong impression from her expressions.

* * * * * * *

At this hour of the night, the ladies' restroom at Wald Med was empty. Drag Thing seated herself on a little stool and spread her paraphernalia out on the counter before her. She sighed. Really, it was much harder than one could imagine, being a woman. Whoever had written that song just didn't know the half of it. The brassiere alone had taken her the longest time to manage, and she had ended up by putting it on backwards and then tugging it around, though at the moment she could see in the mirror that her breasts were decidedly off center.

I will deal with that later, she promised himself. The garters too had gone on backwards. At least the dress, the lovely blue one, had been simpler, though it was a bit snug. It almost seemed as if she had gotten bigger since the night before. She would have to do some alterations before she wore it again.

Never mind. Now for the makeup, she told herself. In her opinion most women just did not get that right. She had always entertained the notion that, given the right opportunity, she could improve upon what she saw on others, and here was her chance. She was dead certain that, when she was done, plenty of women would be envious of what they saw.

When she started on the job, it turned out to be more difficult than she had imagined, though. The moisturizer was simple enough: you just smeared it on, the more the better, but the problems began with the foundation. Despite a liberal

56

application, a five o'clock shadow showed through stubbornly.

She put on a second and then a third coat, and topped it with blush. By this time her face felt gelatinized. For the moment, however, no beard could be seen. That was the important thing, after all.

It will be fine for nighttime, she decided. *Moonlight is always flattering. I will try a different color for day wear. One challenge at a time, that was the sensible approach.*

Her mouth was next. She wanted a symmetrical effect, perfectly balanced. She smeared the color, a vivid coral shade, on her mouth generously and studied her reflection in the mirror.

Hmm. She squinted. Yes, the right side of her mouth was definitely fuller than the left. She added more color to the left side, with exactly the opposite result. She continued adding to first one side and then the other, until she grew alarmed at the size her mouth had become.

I'll do the eyelashes instead, she told herself, confident that they would be easier, *and come back to the mouth when I've got the eyes right.*

The eyelashes turned out to be no easier, unfortunately. The results were horribly streaky. *Hmm,* she thought again. *Maybe the brows. Probably one should get the brows right before tackling the lashes. That made sense, didn't it?*

She penciled the brows in heavily and, on a sudden whim, curled them upward at each end in elaborate curlicues.

Exotic, she thought with a burst of inspiration, grinning broadly at her image in the looking glass. *I have always thought exotic women were especially attractive. I will go exotic.*

Having thus freed herself from the constraints of ordinary make-up, she went to work with a vengeance. More lipstick, more mascara, more eyebrow pencil, still more lipstick. By this time, the foundation looked as if it were cracking, so she slathered on another coat of that as well.

She was really in the spirit of the job now. Delighted with herself, she daubed vivid circles of rouge on her cheeks. *Lovely.* She brightened them up just a bit and applied a beauty spot to one corner of her mouth. Finally she splashed perfume lavishly over her throat and bosom, pausing to read the label: *Nuit d'amour*. French. She did think a little foreign tongue added so much to a romantic moment. She added another generous splash.

I shall go for a smart cocktail, she decided. She felt ready now to face the world outside.

Truth to tell, now that she thought of it, she did feel a bit parched. Maybe she was coming down with something. She frowned, but when she caught sight of her reflection it sent her spirits soaring again.

Definitely exotic. She giggled at her image and blew herself a kiss. *Oh, it's going to be a wonderful night,* she thought, *positively beautiful.*

* * * * * * *

"Some beautiful babe, huh?" Lawrence said.

The three dark-suits watched every move at Caleb Wald's table, their eyes practically boring into Melissa Hyde's back.

"For sure," Curly agreed. He was of a mind just at the moment to agree with anything Lawrence said.

Sylvester, a tall, emaciated-looking man, sniffed and decorously sipped his Shirley Temple through a straw.

"What, you don't like beautiful babes?" Lawrence asked him.

"We are here on business," Sylvester said primly. *Cretins,* he thought. Those two, in his opinion, would sell their souls to get a woman in bed. It made them vulnerable, which was something a Homeland Security agent simply could not afford to be.

Fortunately, he had no such weakness, nor even any time for that sort of thinking. Not that he didn't have sexual urges himself, of course he did. He was certainly normal in that respect, but he did have a customary—and utterly safe— outlet for when the urges got too powerful. One good thing about San Francisco, you could find just about anything you wanted or needed without any problem.

Anyway, the point was, Homeland Security wasn't paying them to indulge their sexual appetites, a fact that he felt had eluded the two next to him, despite the example he tried so hard to set for them. Their mission was far too important to jeopardize with any shenanigans. Behind the thick lenses of his glasses, his eyes remained fixed on the couple at the nearby table. He pursed his lips tightly.

Lawrence and Curly exchanged amused glances. Curly wore a ring in one ear lobe which, with his shiny shaved head, thick neck and burly build, made him look like Mister Clean come to life. Lawrence had hair in abundance, dark ringlets that framed what might have been a handsome face but for his piggish, mean-looking eyes and thin, severe lips.

Underneath the table, his groping hand found Curly's and gave it a firm squeeze. Curly farted noisily. *Pffft.* Sudden excitement always did that to him. This particular excitement had started just the night before, when a mix-up in hotel reservations had put him and Lawrence into the same room together, a room with only one king-sized bed. The excitement, as it turned out, had lasted nearly the entire night, and it was still very much with him. Remembering, he farted again.

The other two pretended not to notice the sound or the acrid smell that wafted upward. At a table next to them, two young women in brightly colored tank tops and hair the color of daffodils wrinkled their noses, but the Dark Suits ignored them.

Curly squeezed Lawrence's hand back. Sylvester sipped and sniffed, and his mouth did "the chicken thing." Lawrence had told Curly the night before, while they were resting together between what Lawrence had called "training regimens", that when Sylvester pursed his tiny mouth like that, it looked like a chicken's butt hole. They had laughed themselves into a near-stupor over that.

Now Lawrence nudged Curly with an elbow and nodded his head in the direction of Sylvester's puckered mouth. Curly looked and nearly choked on his drink. *PFFFT* again, louder than before.

The two young women at the next table got up, drinks in hand, and moved to the bar.

CHAPTER FIVE

"Drinks, first," Caleb said, signaling for the cocktail waitress. "Gin and tonic, right?"

"I really don't want anything to drink, thank you," Melissa said. "I have to get home."

"To the *über*-dyke?" He did not bother to disguise the acid in his voice.

"I didn't come here to discuss my personal life, either, Caleb," Melissa said coldly. "You assured me this was business. Urgent business."

He was on the verge of a sharp retort, but he bit his tongue and managed a smile, one of his special smiles that had always melted her resolve in the past. "I don't want to quarrel with you, Melissa," he said. "I never wanted to quarrel with you. I much preferred having fun. And we did have fun, didn't we?"

"Caleb…." Her voice held a warning note.

"Just say we had fun." He turned the heat up on the smile.

She studied the smile, *that smile*, and to her surprise it left her cold. She looked long and hard at him, her eyes searching his face. In the past, she had thought him the sexiest man alive. He was good looking, there was no denying that, but she saw now that there was something too superficial about his attractiveness. From the precise way he kept his hair glued in place to the calculation she could now read in his smile, nothing was natural, everything too studied.

With a sense of discovery she realized that she had been blind in the past, blinded by her own need. It was a relief to see him finally as he really was and not as she had romantically imagined him. It gave her a tremendous sense of re-

60

lease. How had she ever missed all this before? What a fool she had been. And Janet had been entirely right.

She sighed aloud and said, "Yes, I suppose we did have fun. We must have, or I would not have put up with all the rest, would I? But that's not important now, that's ancient history. Let's cut to the business. What was so important that you had to see me tonight, alone, here?"

Bitch, he wanted to say, *Don't give me any of your crap, if you know what's good for you.*

Instead, he managed to get his expression under control. Romantic had not worked. He switched instead to needy. "The Alley Thing Project," he said in his most earnest voice. "I need some results, Melissa. Where are we with that? Are we anywhere close to wrapping things up?"

She looked away from him, down at the cocktail-scarred table. "I'm afraid not," she said. "We've run into some complications, to be perfectly honest."

The cocktail waitress set another Chivas Regal on the rocks in front of Caleb. He counted out the money for the tab, and added a dime and a nickel for a tip, which the waitress pocketed with a barely concealed sneer. Caleb ignored that and waited until she had gone.

"What kind of complications?" he asked, taking a big swallow of his drink. He did not want to hear about complications. He wanted results.

"Unforeseen ones. Serious ones." She met his eyes again. "It's the genetic threads, they seem to be...."

"I don't need the technical details," he snapped. *And I wouldn't understand them anyway*, he thought. And thought, too, angrily, that she knew that already. She was doing it again, trying to lord her smarts over him. "Just tell me where we are. What is the goddam problem?"

"She Cat is the problem," she said. "She has grown into a monster, a Franken-pussy. She's enormous, and she eats her potential mates. I mean, eats them, literally, rips them to shreds and devours them the moment we put them into the cage with her. Before they even try to mate with her. Before they even have a chance to try. It's as if she hates them simply because they're male."

That much he knew already from his snooping, though he was not going to tell her so.

"Go on," he said when she paused. "I still don't see the problem."

"Well, the truth is, it is getting worse every day, Caleb," Melissa said. "I'm not sure as things stand now that we are even going in the right direction with this. It's becoming too dangerous. Certainly She Cat is becoming too dangerous. I think we might have to kill the project."

"Kill the project?" He glanced at the dark-suited men behind her and realized he had spoken too loudly. Leaning across the table toward her, he said more quietly, "What in name of heaven do you mean, kill the project? We can't kill it now. The backers wouldn't let us."

"Backers?" She gave him a sharp glance. "What do you mean, backers? You never said anything to me about backers."

He shrugged and offered her his naughty-little-boy smile, the one that *never* failed to work. "I didn't want you to worry about that end of things," he said. "Your job is to make things happen in the lab. My job is to run the business. And for a project like Alley Thing, we needed outside money. Even you must realize we've dropped a fortune into the research. If I told you how much you simply would not believe me, but take my word for it, it is a fortune, and not a small one, either."

"Whose fortune is it, then? Who are these mysterious backers that I've not heard of before?" Melissa demanded.

"Who do you think?" he said sharply. "Who else would have a fortune to spend on warfare research?"

"Warfare?" Melissa stared at him, bewildered. "Alley Thing is not about warfare, except on male predators. Why…oh, you must mean the government." Her voice went up. "Is *that* what you are trying to tell me, that I have been conducting some kind of warfare research for the government?" She thought for a moment longer. "For the United States Military?"

"Keep your voice down," he said in a rasping whisper. "Melissa, for God sake, don't act like a child. Do you think anyone but you and your lezzy friend care if a guy jumps a

woman from time to time? In case you didn't know, that is
what men do and it is what women are there for, for Christ's
sake. Why would anyone spend billions to prevent that?
Hell, if that were so damned important, we could just issue
chastity belts to all the women in the world. The truth is, that
would be a helluva lot cheaper than this project has been,
believe me."

"Then what do you mean, warfare?" Melissa shook her
head, still confused. "I do not see where or how warfare
comes into it."

"Use your fucking brain, why don't you? You are supposed to be so smart, figure it out. I saw the possibility the
moment you first suggested the proposal to me, it flashed
before my eyes in an instant: an army of women, turned into
amazons, tougher than any man and fearlessly aggressive,
like She Cat—what man's army could stand up to that? Most
men would back away rather than go hand-to-hand with a
woman. It would change the nature of warfare forever. That
is what they are spending their money for, and now they
want to see some of what they are spending the money on."

Melissa pushed her chair back from the table with a loud
scraping noise and stood abruptly. "I will not be a party to
this, Caleb" she said, her voice rising. "I will not let my project be used for any such purpose."

He glowered furiously at her and she realized that he
was showing his true feelings for the first time since she had
arrived. It was not a pretty sight, but she took a definite
pleasure in realizing that, though it frightened her, his anger
did not cow her as it would have done in the past.

"Haven't you learned anything from the time we spent
together?" he asked in a voice dripping with menace.

"Absolutely," she replied in a frosty tone. "I have
learned that the hokey-pokey is *not* what it's all about."

"I warn you...."

"No," she interrupted him, "I warn you, Caleb Wald,
you will not use my research this way. I will destroy everything first if I must, all the records, all the trials, every last
shred of it, before I will let you use it this way." She turned
to go but paused to add, "And another thing, by the way:
your nose is too big."

She stormed out of the bar. At the nearby booth, the three government agents were already getting to their feet. With a feeble grin, Caleb signaled to them that he had the situation under control. They sat back down reluctantly, and Caleb hurried after Melissa.

Patsy Cline went *Crazy* on the jukebox.

* * * * * * *

That crazy bitch! Caleb swore under his breath as he hastily followed Melissa from the bar.

Outside, the legendary San Francisco fog had descended with a vengeance, muting the flickering yellow and green, green and yellow of the neon lights to pastel swirls that eddied around Melissa where she stood near the curb, talking in a low voice on her cell phone.

He did not know who she was talking to—more than likely it was that lesbian bitch girl friend, Janet Jackle—but, regardless of who it was, he did not want her talking to anybody about what he had just divulged—it was top secret information, for Christ's sake—until he had her safely in line.

He rushed up to her and snatched the phone out of her hand and tossed it violently aside. It hit the sidewalk with a clatter and a bang and some metallic piece flew into the air.

"How dare you?" she sputtered. Her eyes flashed with anger but he saw a flicker of fear in them as well and it fueled his rage. "What right have you to…?"

"No, how dare you?" he snarled. "Listen, you stupid bitch, I have got too much riding on this deal to let you and your lezzy friend mess things up for me. Alley Thing is going to make a rich man out of me, and you're going to help make that happen. You will do what I tell you to do, or else."

"Or else what?" she demanded. "I am not afraid of you anymore, Caleb. And smashing my phone won't do you any good. I was talking to Janet just now. You know as well as I do that she will be here in matter of minutes, and you can be sure you won't intimidate her."

"Then we will just have to get our little disagreement resolved before she gets here, won't we?" he said.

64

He grabbed her arm and gave it a vicious twist. Despite her struggles, he dragged her ruthlessly into the alley that ran alongside the bar, knocking over a garbage can in their scramble. A pair of large gray rats scrambled out of it and disappeared into the darkness "I am telling you, Melissa, you are going to bring me results on this project, at once, and you are going to make those results what I want."

He yanked her arm up behind her back and was pleased to see her grimace in pain. Despite his anger, it gave him a jolt of sexual excitement. He loved making a woman hurt, especially one who would not do what he wanted her to do. There was something ultra-satisfying in teaching them who was boss.

To his surprise, though, she did not cave in as he fully expected her to. Instead, she threw back her head and began to scream loudly, "Help! Help!"

His temper boiled over. *How dare the arrogant bitch try to make him look bad?* He'd see she didn't do any more yelling. He brought back his hand and swung, striking her with all his might. *Wham!* She staggered backward from the blow, took a couple of reeling steps before she tripped over the spilled garbage can and fell hard to the ground. Her head hit the pavement with a loud *thunk,* like the sound of a melon bursting, and she went out like a light.

"Stupid bitch," he muttered, shaking his hand. It actually hurt from the force of the blow. She owed him for that, too, hurting his hand. "You asked for it."

"Excuse me." Someone tapped him on the shoulder.

"Huh?" He had not heard or seen anyone approach. He jumped and looked over his shoulder, and saw the biggest, the freakiest looking drag queen he had ever set eyes upon. She could have been Godzilla in a cheesy blue dress, with a cheap blonde wig on her head that looked more like Christmas tinsel than hair and her mouth painted a neon orange-red. And what in God's name was that perfume that assailed his nostrils: Eau de Sewer?

"Who the hell are you?" he demanded, anger replacing his surprise. However big she was, and however outlandish, she was still just a drag queen.

She smiled a clownish smile at him and said—simpered really—"My name is Thing. Drag Thing." She gave the tinsel hair a coquettish fluff.

He stared at her in bewilderment. *Drag Thing? What kind of a fucking name was that?*

"Well, get this, Miss Thing," he said aloud, "Why don't you butt out and mind your own frigging business." He jabbed a finger at her immense bosom.

She lightly swatted his finger away and giggled. "Man slapping woman around *is* Drag Thing's business. Man is being naughty. Drag Thing does not like men who are mean to women."

"Yeah? Well how would you like some of what she's getting?" he demanded in a threatening voice. He could slap drag queens around just as well as women, was how he saw it, even big, freaky ones.

He drew his fist back to punch her a good one, but before he could swing it, she struck him alongside the head with a purse the size—and feel—of a Volkswagen bus. *Pow!*

It was his turn to go down for the count. He hit the sidewalk hard.

* * * * * * *

Drag Thing put her hands on her hips and surveyed the scene. There was no question that the naughty man was out like a light. And the woman gave no signs of waking either.

There was a cell phone lying on the sidewalk, near the woman. Drag Thing went to it and picked it up. The cover had broken off but, yes, when she hit the "talk" button, she got a dial tone. It was still working, then. She punched in the emergency number for the police.

"Emergency," a voice answered on the other end of the line.

"Hello? Is that the police?" Drag Thing said into the phone. "Well, I was just taking a little stroll around the neighborhood, and I happened to discover these two people lying unconscious on the sidewalk. No, I don't know what happened to them. Where? Oh, they are just outside a bar. What's that? Well, wait a minute, let me see here: it's called

The Copa Club, now isn't that the sweetest? Where is it? Oh, it's on Hayes, Hayes and...hmm, Laguna, I think. Oh, dear, just send somebody by, won't you, please, they couldn't possibly miss them. How many people could there be lying about on the sidewalk at this hour of the night? Well, yes, of course, I know this is San Francisco, but still.... What's that? My name? Oh, that doesn't matter, does it? I am just your friendly neighborhood Drag Thing."

She pushed the "off" button on the phone and placed it carefully by the unconscious woman, and looked around, not quite sure what she should do next.

It was the bar's festive green and yellow lights that had initially drawn her in this direction, and it had been her plan to go in and order herself a little refreshment. She was ever so thirsty. She felt downright parched, in fact. As if she had a fever. And there was an odd buzzing noise somewhere back in her mind, like a wasp in a hot attic. Yes, definitely, a drink was what she needed.

Now, however, she supposed the sensible thing to do would be to remove herself from the scene of the crime, so to speak, as expeditiously as possible. The police would take care of things here. They would arrest the naughty man and see that the woman got medical attention. And, really, she would just be in the way, wouldn't she?

She started to move on but she had gone only a few feet however, when a wicked thought occurred to her and she came to a halt, considering it more fully.

She smiled to herself, a wide grin that filled her face with bright red, overlarge lips. She went back to the unconscious man and, stooping down, reached inside his jacket and took his wallet from the inside pocket. It was positively stuffed with money.

She removed a handful of bills without counting them and tossed the wallet with the rest of the money to the ground beside him. She still owed that shop for her makeup, after all, and she liked to pay her debts.

And it wasn't like she was stealing his money, either. "That," she said with a clear sense of justice, stuffing the money into her purse, "Is the fine Drag Thing assesses you for being naughty. Those who prey, must pay. It's only right."

Taking yet another look at his face, she had a feeling that she knew the man, but she could not immediately place him. She studied his face intently, and as she did so, another idea just leaped into her mind out of nowhere, one that made her giggle mischievously. Kneeling on the pavement beside him, she opened her purse and began to rummage in it.

I must hurry, she told herself, *before the police people come, or the naughty man wakes up.*

* * * * * * *

Caleb Wald woke up with a start and a major headache. He struggled to a sitting position, shaking his head to clear it, and, remembering, looked around in alarm. Luckily, that frightening drag apparition was gone. *Jesus almighty*, he thought. He had never been hit so hard in his life. She must have had a cement block in that damned purse.

Something caught his eye and he realized his wallet was lying on the pavement beside him. That fucking freak had robbed him while he was out. He reached for the wallet and at the same time he saw Melissa lying a few feet away in a pile of garbage. For a moment he could not think why she was sprawled on the pavement like that. Then it came back to him, the entire scene: he had hit her and she had fallen, banging her head hard on the pavement.

Worried, he half crawled over to where she was. Up close, he could see there was a little pool of nearly dried blood around her head and she did not appear to be breathing.

He felt a mounting sense of panic. Christ, he had killed her. Breathing heavily, he scrambled to his feet and started to run, to get away before anybody found him in an alley with a dead woman.

At the street, however, he paused in the flickering yellow and green light to reconsider what he should do. First, it would not do him any good to take off, would it? A dozen or more people must have seen him with her in the bar earlier, would have seen her storm out in a huff, too, and had seen him go after her. Running away now would only make him look all the more guilty, wouldn't it? It wasn't as if people couldn't identify him to the cops when they came. He had to think of some better angle.

You've got to think, he told himself frantically. *Figure it out, Caleb. You're smarter than anyone else. You can find a way out of this.*

He thought of that grotesque faggot who had knocked him silly: Drag Thing, she had called herself. If she cracked him in the head with something and knocked him cold, why couldn't she just as well have been the one who whacked Melissa?

They could examine him, he was sure, and confirm that he had been knocked out. Hell, if nothing else, he must have a bump on his head the size of an Idaho potato. He felt to confirm it. Yes, there was a lump, and it was a lulu. Anyone checking it out would know he had been knocked cold. Who was to say whether Melissa had been killed before or after he was cold-cocked? No one could accuse an unconscious man of harming anybody.

Brilliant! Sometimes it was almost scary how sharp he was. He headed for the bar and as he rushed through the door, he staggered like a man who was only semi-conscious. "Help," he yelled, holding his head, "Somebody call the cops. We've been mugged."

Of course his entrance got everyone's attention. He couldn't have timed it better. The jukebox was momentarily silent. All eyes were immediately upon him.

To his astonishment, however, people began to laugh. He looked in the direction of the dark suited trio of Homeland Security agents. They were on their feet, and amazingly Curly and Lawrence were laughing the hardest of all. Even that super-prissy Sylvester had a smirk on his face.

"What the hell?" Caleb said aloud, baffled. He went to the bar and looked into the smoky mirror behind the stacked liquor bottles. At first, in the dim light, it was difficult to see more than a ghostly image. He leaned closer across the bar and squinted at the glass.

What he saw was a face covered with make-up: a crimson lipsticked mouth, with enormous smears of rouge on his cheeks and eyes fairly dripping with mascara. It was his face, but it had been transformed into a ludicrous parody of a woman's made-up face. That frigging bitch had painted him while he was unconscious.

He swore aloud and started for the john, to wash the makeup off. People were still laughing as he went by. He grabbed one little twit by the lapels. "What's so damn funny?" he demanded.

The twit paled and his laughter died in his throat. "N-nothing," he stammered, his eyes wide.

Caleb shoved him aside. "Then shut the fuck up, why don't you?"

He pointed a finger at the bartender. "Call the cops," he said. "There's a dead woman outside." Murder in his heart, he charged into the restroom.

"Drag Thing. I'll kill that freak," he vowed to his reflection. He turned the water on full and began to scrub at his face.

* * * * * * *

A few blocks away Drag Thing caught sight of her reflection in a plate glass window and paused to look critically at herself.

Yes, the dress was definitely an improvement over her previous costume. It really was a lovely shade of blue. *It brings out the color of my eyes,* she thought with satisfaction.

It was a little Spartan for her tastes, though. Maybe if they added some bows, or a ruffle here and there. And sequins, tons of sequins, she did so adore sequins. She would have to take all this up with the dress's designer. They really must talk soon.

Something occurred to her suddenly. The face looking back at her from the glass was only vaguely familiar. Oughtn't she to recognize her own face? Though when she tried, she could not quite summon up an image of what her face was supposed to look like.

It was hard for her, however, to stay focused on anything for long. The way her thoughts swirled around inside her head it was a wonder she wasn't spinning like a top. She blew the image in the glass a kiss and went on. What did it matter, really, if she recognized herself or not? She knew who she was, and when you came down to it, that was what was most important. She was Drag Thing. What a lovely name!

And what a lovely night it was, too. She took a deep breath of the cool damp air and began to hum and then to skip merrily along the sidewalk, and finally she executed a somewhat clumsy pirouette.

Just like the animals in that Disney film, she thought, *I dearly do love that movie.* Only, of course, those hippos in the movie had partners to help them. You really could not do a decent pirouette unaided. Where were the crocogators when you most needed them?

Undaunted, she did an entire series of giddy spins into the street. A police car, red lights flashing, suddenly emerged from the fog, bearing down upon her. She leaped back out of its way just in time, the car narrowly missing her.

The black and white stopped sharply with a squeal of tires on pavement and a window came down. "Hey, you," the uniformed woman behind the wheel shouted. "Hold on there. You could have gotten yourself killed, you know, dancing in the street like that."

"It's all right, officer," Drag Thing called back without stopping, and blew her a quick kiss, "I forgive you. I love police peoples." She began to skip and twirl again and in a moment had vanished, still dancing, into the night.

Teri Warren stared open-mouthed after her. "Did you get a good look at that?" she asked her partner.

"Weird," Jake Martin agreed. "Should we check her out, you think?"

Teri considered that for a second, and shook her head. "We're on a call. Someone murdered, the caller said. Anyway, except for dancing out in front of a police car and looking awfully peculiar, this one didn't do anything illegal that I could see."

Something was nagging at the back of her mind, however, as she put the car in gear again. She hesitated, and Jake lifted an eyebrow. After a moment, Teri frowned and shrugged, and continued on toward The Copa Club.

DRAG THING, BY VICTOR J. BANIS

A gentle rain had begun to fall.

* * * * * * *

San Francisco summers are mostly rainless, so that by the time the first showers arrive in the fall, the locals are as glad for them as the thirsty earth is.

Drag Thing was certainly glad for the rain. She turned her painted face up to the cool droplets. They seemed to wash a feverish heat from her brow. *Had she been ill,* she wondered? She couldn't quite remember. She certainly did feel peculiar, though. And she was so thirsty. She stuck her tongue out full length and savored the tickle of raindrops on it.

"I love all peoples," she said aloud, and quickly amended, "except some peoples."

Life was delicious! She laughed gaily, spun into another pirouette, and like one of the hippos in that film, performed an astonishing *jeté* across a looming puddle.

CHAPTER SIX

"All I know is she was some kind of freak," Caleb told the female cop. "She called herself Drag Thing."

"Drag Thing?" Teri's eyes widened.

Caleb peered suspiciously at her. "Do you know her?" he asked.

"No. But there have been some funny stories circulating…." Teri's thoughts flashed back to the drag queen those street punks had described to her the night before, and to the peculiar creature she and Jake had encountered dancing through the fog a few minutes ago. She had a feeling that they might have just crossed paths with the mysterious Drag Thing.

Her partner had the same idea. "Do you think…?" Jake started to say, but Teri interrupted him with a shake of her head. She wasn't quite sure why, but she did not want to share that possibility with the man in front of her.

"So, what exactly were you and the lady doing when this Drag Thing came up?" she asked instead.

"We were just standing here outside the bar, talking," Caleb said, his expression a picture of innocence. "You know, her place or mine, that sort of thing."

She studied him with a vague sense of suspicion. Something about this guy rubbed her the wrong way. He was good looking, she supposed, if you liked the lounge lizard type, with too pale skin and too perfectly colored hair that ought to have shown at least a strand or two of gray to judge from the lines around his eyes. And there was that beak of a nose…*I'll bet he thinks it looks noble*, she thought wryly.

His story didn't seem quite right either. His face was freshly washed, his hair still damp where it lay glued too prettily to his brow. Did a man who was just mugged and woke up to discover his lady friend had been killed, rush to wash his face first thing, and arrange his hair? And there was a smear of red on his collar—not blood, but lipstick, she thought, or it might have been rouge.

He followed her glance and saw it too. "It was a very friendly conversation," he said with a smarmy grin. She noticed that when he smiled, his lips forgot to inform his eyes. In her book, the guy was definitely a creepo.

"Then what happened?" she asked coldly.

"Then what happened will amaze you," he said. "This thing, Drag Thing, she came up out of nowhere, I didn't even see her approach, and without any warning or any provocation, she started swinging. She just swatted Melissa there like she was a tennis ball, must have knocked her ten feet before she landed. So, I started to try to help her, you know, like a guy is supposed to do. I said, 'hey, you can't slap a woman around like that,' and the next thing I know I am waking up on the pavement. She must have hit me with a rock. Plus, she stole my money while I was out."

They were interrupted by an abrupt squeal of rubber on pavement and a red Mustang slid to a stop at the curb. A tall, wild looking woman with spiky orange hair leaped out of the car and ran toward them. Before Teri could react, the woman had attacked Caleb Wald.

"You filthy scum," Janet Jackle shrieked, clawing at his eyes, "You rotten piece of shit. What have you done to my Melissa?"

"Get her off me," Caleb yelled, frantically trying to protect himself.

It was all Teri and Jake could do to get the two separated. "Who are you?" Teri demanded when they finally had them apart.

"Janet Jackle. I'm Melissa's partner. She called me and said that he was…." For the first time she looked past them and saw the paramedic and the EMT kneeling over Melissa. She let out another scream. "Melissa! You've killed her!" She renewed her efforts to get at her nemesis.

"She's not dead," EMT Luis Cordero, said.

There was a sudden loud explosive noise, like a string of firecrackers going off, *pop, pop, pop.* Teri dropped into a defensive crouch, her hand going automatically to her gun.

"What the hell?" she said, looking around for their attacker.

After a second or two, Jake sniffed the air and grimaced. "Someone farted. I mean, really farted," he said.

"Jesus, you aren't kidding." Teri wrinkled her nose in disgust at the noxious cloud enveloping them.

"She's alive?" Wald asked in a tremulous voice, so alarmed by that news that he hardly even noticed Curly's odiferous contribution to the scene.

"Just barely. She seems to be in a coma, though," the paramedic said.

"You did this, you bastard," Janet cried, struggling even more fervently to get at Caleb.

"No, not me." Wald backed away even though Jake still held her firmly. "Like I just told the cop lady there, it was this giant drag queen that hit her. Drag Thing, she calls herself."

"Liar!"

"It's true," a male voice said from nearby.

Teri looked in the direction of the voice and saw a man in a black suit—three men in identical black suits, actually. Two of them were enormous, bull-muscled characters who would have looked more at home in wrestling trunks. The one who stepped forward, though, the one who had spoken, was an Ichabod Crane look-alike, with thick glasses and a funny little mouth that reminded her of something, although she could not at the moment think what that was.

"What he says is true," Sylvester said. "We saw it happen, my friends and I. We were driving by and we saw this man and the woman talking, all friendly like, and suddenly this enormous woman—well, she was dressed like a woman, anyway, but I daresay she did not really look like one, not like any woman I have ever seen—anyway, she came out of the fog without any warning and jumped all over them, swinging her pocketbook like a deadly weapon. I am surprised she didn't kill them both. It was quite alarming, really."

75

"What did you do when you saw this assault taking place?" Teri asked.

He shrugged. "We wanted to help, of course," he said, "You know, good Samaritans, and all that. But by the time we found a place to park the car and came back, the woman was already unconscious and he was in the bar looking for help. And the drag queen had gone."

"Where did she go?" Teri asked.

He shook his head. "It's hard to say, with all this fog. She just disappeared, like a wisp of smoke," he said.

Pop, pop, pop, just like before. Jake wrinkled his nose again. *Jesus, what a stench*, he thought. This guy had a serious problem.

"See, it's just like I told you," Caleb said. He was relieved that the government boys had stepped in to alibi him; but the news that Melissa was alive was a real downer. When she recovered, she would give the lie to his story.

If, he quickly amended. *If she recovered*. He'd just somehow have to make sure that didn't happen.

Janet had stopped struggling with the two police officers but the look she gave Caleb was no less hate-filled. "What did you say she called herself?" she asked, "this attacker thing of yours?"

"Drag Thing," Caleb said. "And, believe me, she is no thing of mine."

The medics had managed to get Melissa onto a stretcher and they started with her toward the waiting ambulance.

"Let me go, I'm not going to hurt him. I could care less about him," Janet said, struggling once again to free herself. "I'm going with her."

Teri and Jake exchanged glances. After a moment's hesitation, Teri nodded and Jake let go of her. Janet hurried after the two men with the stretcher but before she caught up with them she paused to look back and say, "And then I'm going to find this Drag Thing, the one who did this to her."

"Look," Teri said, "There'll be no vigilante nonsense. Leave this to the police."

"That's our job," Jake added.

"Take my word for it, I am going to make it my job. I am going to find Drag Thing and when I do, I swear I am going to kill him, whoever she or he is," Janet said.

"Not if I beat you to it," Caleb said.

Janet gave him a look of pure loathing. It was hard to imagine her and this bastard sharing a common goal. "No," she said emphatically, "he's mine." Without waiting for a reply, she climbed into the ambulance after the stretcher. In a moment it was on its way, siren wailing, lights flashing.

"Whew," Teri said, shaking her head. "What a screwy mess."

"Who do you suppose this Drag Thing is?" Jake asked.

"Who—or what?"

"Oh, oh." Jake looked over her shoulder as a van pulled up to the curb. "Channel 2 News, on the scene."

"You deal with them," Teri said, "I'm going to get some statements."

When she turned toward the three men in the black suits, however, they were gone. Caleb Wald stood alone. "Where did they go?" she asked him.

He gave her a blank look. "They just vanished. Into the alley, maybe. Like that Drag Thing."

* * * * * * *

Every trace of Alley Thing had been destroyed: records, samples, slides, compact discs, even the hard drive from the computer. The laboratory counters and the floors were littered with broken glass and shredded paper. The sinks were filled with the ashes of burnt documents and journals. Blood samples, sera, everything liquid, had gone down the drains. The room positively reeked with the acrid stench of chemicals and smoke and electrical short circuits.

Janet did not know exactly what it was that Caleb had done that had so angered Melissa. The telephone connection had been broken before Melissa could tell her that. She did know, however, that it had been Melissa's intention to destroy the project. That much Melissa had managed to tell her on the phone. "I'm going to destroy everything, every trace of Alley Thing," she had said. "There must be no trace of our

77

research left for Caleb to find. The formula will exist no-where but in my mind, where he will never find it."

Which told Janet as well that whatever Caleb had been up to, it must have been nefarious indeed, for Melissa to decide on anything so drastic as the destruction of her pet project.

The last thing Melissa had said, her very last word before the phone connection had been lost, was, "Warfare."

Janet could not begin to comprehend what that meant. She could not see how their project was in any way connected to warfare. Nevertheless, on the ride to the hospital two hours earlier, she had vowed to an unconscious Melissa that she would carry out her wish.

She had done so with a vengeance. Two years of diligent, seemingly endless work, all those nights working late here in the lab, had been erased, destroyed completely. But it was worth it to Janet just to imagine when the loathsome Caleb Wald came here later, as she had no doubt he would do, and discovered what she had done.

"Take that, you bastard," she muttered aloud. "You'll reap no profits from my Melissa's misery."

Only two things were left for her to deal with: She Cat, watching with intense interest from her cage, and the vial with the last of their B test serum, the serum that had caused such startling changes in the creature.

She found a syringe in a drawer and carefully filled it with the remains of the serum. For just a moment she hesitated. She knew that she was taking an enormous risk, without any clue as to what the final consequences might be. The serum had never been tried on a human subject, and certainly, the results with She Cat were enough to give one pause. How a human would react to it was anyone's guess.

To her way of thinking, however, she had no alternative. She had a job to do, and that job was going to require something more than her ordinary woman's strength. She had made the unconscious Melissa another promise as well.

"I swear to you, I will get him," she had vowed while she wept silently, holding her beloved's hand. "I will find this Drag Thing, and I will make him pay for what he has done to you."

Just thinking of her darling, lying helpless and uncon-scious in a hospital bed, made her heart ache with anguish. Was she in pain? Was she aware of her surroundings? *Did she hear my vows?*

"I must go to her," she said aloud. "I must tell her that her wishes have been carried out." As soon as she had fin-ished here.

But first...she put the tip of the syringe against her arm. Her hand shook. She paused, contemplating in dread what she was about to do. There was no telling what would hap-pen, no way of knowing what the serum might do to her, and no way of undoing her actions once they were done. They had never yet even thought of an antidote to the serum. She knew that Melissa would tell her she was being rash, reck-less, even, courting unknown danger.

I must, she swore silently. *It's the only way. I must do this,* she told herself yet again.

She gritted her teeth with determination and resolutely plunged the syringe into her arm. There was an immediate sensation of heat, starting at the injection site and spreading swiftly up her arm. It felt as if her veins were on fire, a blaze that shot up her arm and her shoulder in quick succession, and through her entire body.

Oddly, she welcomed the burn even as it flamed through her. Whatever happened to her, she was confident of one thing: she would be far stronger afterward than she had ever been before, stronger and more aggressive, and she would need that strength, and that disposition, to do what she had to do. Even as she thought that, she seemed to feel stronger al-ready, physically more confident, as if she could tackle any-thing, anyone.

"Now then, Miss Drag Thing," she said aloud, grinning fiercely, "Let me tell you something, bitch: you can swap your frocks and you can trim your tresses, but you can not hide from me. You are out there somewhere and I will find you, I swear it. I will make you pay for what you have done."

There was one last thing still that she must do. She had put it off for as long as she could, but she could avoid it no longer. Tears welled up in her eyes as she turned to She Cat's cage.

From within the cage, She Cat watched her warily. Oddly, for the first time in all these months, Janet regarded the animal with a sense of affection. The cat had been Melissa's. In a sense, She Cat was the child of Melissa's brilliant research. Destroying her seemed almost like a betrayal, and so cruel.

She could not leave the cat here, however, for Caleb Wald to find. He would only need to draw some blood and have it analyzed to have the Alley Thing formula at his disposal. At all costs, she must not allow that to happen. Whatever he was up to, and she had no doubt he was up to something nefarious, his schemes must be thwarted.

Looking at the cat, a vague memory stirred in her mind. What was that poem she had always liked as a child? She thought a moment, dredging her memory. A cat...a pussycat...pussy....

It came to her in a flash, and she recited in a loud voice, "The owl looked up to the stars above, and sang to a small guitar, O lovely pussy, O pussy my love, what a beautiful pussy you are, you are, what a beautiful pussy you are."

Sudden inspiration struck her. No, she would not destroy the cat. She Cat *had* been Melissa's child, her brilliant creation. Now she would be her creator's avenger.

"You are going to help me find him," she told the watching beast. She opened the door of the cage. Instead of attacking the way she usually did, She Cat sat unmoving, as if she had understood Janet's words and was waiting to see what would happen next.

Janet reached inside with the vial and upturned it, and sprinkled the last few drops of the serum over the cat's head.

"I christen thee Missy," she intoned in a somber voice. "That was my darling's suggestion, do you remember, Missy? From this moment forward, you will be Missy Hyde."

Far from being annoyed by the drops that fell upon her, the newly named Missy Hyde seemed to understand and approve of what Janet was saying. She licked a droplet from one whisker and made a sound that might have been a purr or the distant rumble of a subway train.

On an impulse, Janet seized the cage from the counter and, hugging it to her bosom, spun around lightly. "What a beautiful pussy you are, you are, what a beautiful pussy you are," she sang. Missy Hyde added an enthusiastic yowl to the chorus.

Janet paused to crush the now empty serum vial under her foot with a pop and took one final glance around. It felt to her like she had already grown taller. She seemed to be looking down on things from a different perspective, and the cage that had been heavy a moment before now felt as light as paper. Overflowing with new-found confidence, she strode briskly to the door.

"Ready or not, Drag Thing," she said, flinging the door open with a violence that sent it crashing against the wall, "here come Dr. Jackle and Missy Hyde."

But first, she must tell Melissa what she had done, and introduce her to Missy Hyde. She must go to Melissa—to the hospital.

* * * * * * *

Gladys Kravitz—Nurse Kravitz here in her domain— came along the hospital corridor with a full bedpan in her hands and saw that the light was on in Room 812, a faint sliver of yellow showing under the door.

That is odd, she thought. *That patient is in a coma, why would she have a light on in the wee small hours of the morning?* Besides, she was sure the light had not been on when she had gone by just a few minutes earlier. The door had not been closed then, either, she realized, as it was now. As it should not be. A violation of hospital regulations, regulations it was her sworn duty to uphold.

She pushed the door open and stepped cautiously into the room. It was only the bedside light that was on, and its pale yellow glow left most of the room in shadow. At first, she did not see anyone. Then with a start she realized that there was a man in bed with the patient, cradling her in his arms. As she gaped in astonishment, he sobbed softly and whispered something to the unconscious woman.

"What are you doing?" Nurse Kravitz demanded angrily. She brooked no hanky-panky on her shift and it was well past visiting hours.

He half sat up. It was not a man after all, she realized belatedly, but a woman, an enormous woman—indeed, a devilish parody of womanhood in huge baggy overalls and a voluminous sweat shirt that for all their considerable size both nevertheless managed to look too small for her immense body. Her hair was a wiry tangle of copper, her angry eyes flashed in the dim light with green fire. Nurse Kravitz's flesh crawled as those eyes fell upon her, and the bedpan sloshed in her hands.

"Get out," the woman said. "Leave us alone."

"I will not," Nurse Kravitz replied stoutly, summoning her resolve. Years of nursing often-irascible patients had made her steadfast in the performance of her duty. She had weathered every possible type of crisis and she was not about to be intimidated, not even by this ferocious gargoyle.

"Don't make me show you my pussy," the woman on the bed said, her voice a raspy snarl.

Nurse Kravitz's cheeks flamed. "Don't be crude," she snapped, but even as she said this, something stirred in the darkness by the bed. "What's that?" she demanded. She sniffed the air. "Have you brought an animal into this room? Hospital regulations forbid…."

A chain clinked noisily and a shadow separated itself from the other shadows on the floor and slunk toward her. A cat, Nurse Kravitz thought—or some kind of feline, but it was far too large, she realized at a second glance, to be an ordinary house cat. It was the size of a small collie, its unkempt fur orange and white and black. And it smelled, it positively reeked, the ugly scent of wet, dirty hair and something else. The smell of blood—the unsettling thought jumped into her mind.

The animal advanced a step or two further in her direction. The chain that tethered the monstrous beast to the bed clinked again as it reached its full length. Nurse Kravitz stared, frozen in horror as the monster cat regarded her with eyes a malevolent yellow-green.

The woman on the bed sat up and grinned wickedly at her. "I warned you, you pestiferous old bitch," she cried. "Here you are, Missy, go show the nurse lady what a beautiful pussy you are, you are, what a beautiful pussy you are."

She, laughed, a witch's cackle, and reached down to unclasp the chain. In happy anticipation, the cat curled her lips back to reveal teeth that would have done a shark proud and crouched, ready to leap.

With a shriek of terror, Nurse Kravitz dropped the bedpan she was holding and ran for her life. A mocking laugh and a beastly howl pursued her along the corridor.

* * * * * * *

Peter laughed in bitter disappointment when he saw the devastation in the lab. His last hope was dashed.

They were gone. Everything was gone: women, cat, cages. The laboratory was a wreck. Burnt papers, gutted computers and broken vials were strewn everywhere, and the air was foul with the stink of smoke and spilled chemicals.

He stared around the room in dismay. Somehow when he had awakened once more at the apartment, his head splitting, a large part of the night missing from his memory, he had hoped against hope that he would find an answer here, a solution to the fantastic events that were happening to him.

Fragments of glass crunched under his foot as he stepped toward the empty counter where the cat's cage had stood only the night before. What was he to do now? Where was he to turn? What must his next move be?

"Don't move," a voice said behind him.

He spun around to find a trio of dark-suited men filling the office doorway. The man to the forefront was tall and bone thin, while the two behind him were gorillas whose bulging muscles threatened the seams of their cheap suits. One of the gorillas had a gun trained on him, but it was the tall skinny one who appeared to be in charge.

"Who are you?" Peter asked of him. "What are you doing here?"

"That's my line," the tall one said. "Put your hands in the air." Peter did as he was told. "That's better. Now, who exactly are you, and what are *you* doing here?"

"I'm the janitor. I came to clean up." Peter kept his hands obediently in the air, but he had an odd sense of something rising up within him, some elemental force that threatened to take him over.

Not now, he thought desperately, *not here.* He swallowed and tried to breathe deeply, to calm himself. The angry thing within him retreated watchfully.

"I would say it looks like you cleaned up, all right." Sylvester glanced toward the hall doorway. "Do you know this guy?" The trio moved aside and a fourth man stepped into the room.

For a moment, Peter did not recognize him.

"He's the janitor all right." Caleb Wald nodded. He turned to Peter. "Who did this?" he demanded. "Where is she?"

"Who?" Peter asked. "You mean those women doctors? I haven't seen them. I don't understand what this is all about. I came in just a minute ago to clean as usual, and I found the place like this. There was no one here, no one that I saw, until you guys showed up. Can I put my hands down?"

Lawrence glanced at Sylvester, who nodded and motioned for Caleb to come the rest of the way into the room. Caleb's nostrils flared angrily as he looked around at the destruction wrought in the laboratory.

"Alley Thing is destroyed, every bit of it," he spat out. "That bitch! I should have knocked the bejesus out of her instead of the other one." He picked up the cover of a notebook from the floor. Nothing. Every page had been ripped out, probably included in that smoldering pile of ashes in one sink. He flung the plastic binder aside with an angry oath and looked around, his gaze falling on Peter. He had all but forgotten him.

"Get out of here," he ordered.

"I should clean things…."

"He said out," Lawrence insisted and waved the gun menacingly.

"And don't come back, either," Caleb Wald added.

"Does this mean I'm out of a job?" Peter asked in dismay.

"You're lucky you're not out of this world," Wald said. "And if you don't get out of her pretty fast, you may be."

Peter sidled carefully past him and into the hall, half expecting the goons to change their mind and shoot him. Not until he was in the elevator and the door closed did he begin to breathe easily again.

Only for a moment, however. Now that he was out of danger, his anger came to the fore, and with it, that looming sense of another presence inside him, a presence demanding to be released.

Alley Thing. The words sprang into his mind from nowhere. *Drag Thing?*

As if in answer, a voice inside his head seemed to say, *Hello, Bunny.*

Chapter Seven

"Our employers are going to be unhappy," Sylvester told Caleb.

"Very unhappy," Lawrence agreed.

"Pissed," Curly added for emphasis.

Caleb was uncomfortably aware that Lawrence had not put the gun away. He knew these guys played rough. They were Homeland, weren't they? *Jesus, was this prick going to shoot him now?* He looked a question at Sylvester. *And what was it about that one's mouth anyway,* he wondered fleetingly, *it looked funny somehow? What did it remind him of?*

Sylvester saw him look at the gun and motioned for Lawrence to put it away. Lawrence slipped it into the waistband of his trousers; not, Caleb noted, into his holster. It was quicker to grab a gun from the waistband than from a holster. Which only told him that the jerk still might shoot him before they were finished.

"Look," he said, in a placating voice, "Let's go to my office, why don't we? We can talk safely there. Just in case that fruity janitor decided to hang around."

The building that housed Wald-Med Pharmaceuticals had once been an apartment house, and not all of the apartments had been converted to labs and offices. Caleb's office occupied one of the old apartments, still with its separate kitchen and a comfortable sitting area where he entertained visitors and a bedroom where he sometimes entertained women friends.

"Have a seat," he gestured at the dark suits and nodded toward the sofa. "How about something to drink?"

"A beer for me," Lawrence said. He sat on the small sofa and patted the seat for Curly to sit beside him.

At least he put the frigging gun away, Caleb thought with some relief.

"Same for me," Curly said.

"I will have a Shirley Temple," Sylvester sat by himself on one of the straight wooden chairs.

"Sorry, all I've got is Sprite," Caleb said. He went into the kitchen and closed the door carefully behind himself. The lock slid to with a satisfying clink. Remembering the gun and the cold look Sylvester had given him, he flicked on the little television sitting on the kitchen counter. A closed circuit TV gave him a view of the adjoining room and the three men he had just left.

Just in case they mean to sneak up on me, he thought. Across the kitchen another door opened into a back corridor that led to a freight elevator just a few steps away. If he had to, if they tried to pull anything, he could make a fast exit while they were breaking in this door.

What really pissed him was that, what had happened was not in any way his fault. *It was entirely her fault, the bitch*, he thought angrily. Melissa Hyde. She was the one who had betrayed him. She deserved what she had gotten.

But you could just bet these guys were blaming him for everything nevertheless. He would not put it past them to decide to plug him after all, to save their own butts. That was the way the government boys worked. Hard asses, every one of them.

For the moment, though, his guests were seated where he had left them, waiting patiently, not even saying anything to one another. He took three glasses down from a cupboard wiped them on a pant leg and, keeping one eye glued to the television screen, peed carefully into the bottom of two of them and filled them with beer from the refrigerator, carefully so as to keep a good head of foam.

The Sprite was a little more difficult. The best he could do with that was cough up a big wad of phlegm: *honk, hack, grrrmm* and spit it into the glass with the soda pop. He stirred all three glasses carefully, set them on a tray, and brought them back into the sitting area, passing them around.

The gorillas immediately took hearty swigs of the beers he handed them. Sylvester sipped his Sprite decorously.

"No cherry?" he asked.

"Afraid there hasn't been one of those around here for years," Caleb said with a chortle.

"Har, har, har," Curly laughed noisily, but the frowns from the other two quickly silenced him except for a faint *hiss,* like the air leaking out of a tire.

"Gosh, this is good beer," Lawrence said, taking another hearty swig.

Curly slurped and smacked his lips. "Terrif'," he said. "What kind is it?"

"It's a special label. So now what do we do?" Caleb asked.

"It's obvious. Now, you find the woman," Sylvester said. "This Doctor Janet Jackle."

Caleb considered that for a moment. "She must have the cat with her," he said, thinking aloud. "The damn thing is the size of a sheepdog and eats small children, from what Melissa told me. It shouldn't be too hard to find the two of them. A cat that size would be hard to miss. Meantime, there is still the other one, the one in the hospital, Melissa Hyde. She's a problem, too. If she wakes up, she's going to make trouble. She will tell them I was the one who conked her, not that Drag Thing the way I told the cops."

"So, what's the prob'? We just see she doesn't wake up," Curly said.

Which Caleb thought was a good idea, but Sylvester quickly disagreed. "Morons," he said scornfully. "We need her alive. She is the one who can tell us the formula if we can't get it any other way. She is the only one who knows it, right? So we have to see that she stays alive, at least until we get the Alley Thing formula. We just have to make sure we are the ones who are there when she wakes up."

Caleb shook his head. "It won't do any good," he said. "She won't tell me a thing. She's totally pissed at me. The ungrateful bitch. That's why I whacked her in the first place."

"She will tell us, if we make her the right offer," Sylvester said.

"Such as?" Caleb asked.

"Such as, we offer to trade her girlfriend for the formula."

"But we haven't got her girlfriend," Caleb said.

"We will have to get her, then," Sylvester said. "*You* will have to get her, won't you?"

Shit, Caleb thought, *who would ever have dreamed he would want to hook up with Janet Jackle, the über-dyke?*

Sylvester set his Sprite aside and stood up. The gorillas quickly chugged their beers and did the same. "Next time," Sylvester said, "I want a cherry."

"The beer was great," Lawrence said enthusiastically.

"What brand did you say it was?" Curly asked.

"It's a Chinese beer," Caleb said. "Yellow River. It's hard to find."

"I'll look for it," Lawrence said, and Curly nodded eagerly.

Sylvester looked around at the quasi-apartment. "We need to consolidate," he said. "Stay close together till we get this dilemma resolved. Maybe we should move in here with you."

Which Caleb definitely did not want, but he could see no alternative. "There's two other apartments down the hall," he said. "If a couple of you don't mind doubling up, you could move into them."

"I'll take one," Sylvester said. "You two can share the other."

"That's cool," Lawrence said. *Pffft* from Curly.

"I have to tell you, though, they are kind of primitive," Caleb warned. "They've got beds. Refrigerators. Showers. The basics. No television, though, nothing like that."

"We won't be able to watch TV?" Curly asked, dismayed. "I just hate it when I miss Sesame Street?"

"Ah, come on," Lawrence said, giving him a playful punch on his massive shoulder. "We can find ways to occupy ourselves besides TV, can't we?"

With a thunderous roar, Curly let fly a noxious cloud of gas.

"Jesus," Caleb said. "You ought to do something about your condition. Maybe it's diet."

"Yeah, it's probably something you ate recently," Lawrence said.

This time the output was even louder and more malodorous.

Caleb pinched his nose between his fingers and Lawrence laughed. Sylvester single-mindedly ignored the interchange and pursed his lips.

What is about his mouth...? Caleb wondered.

"Find the woman," Sylvester said. "And the cat."

* * * * * * *

"Where are you going with that patient?"

"Transfer," Janet mumbled, keeping her head down so no one could get a good look at her face. She wheeled the bed and the IV trolley into the elevator.

"Wait," the young intern started to say, but Janet pushed the button to close the elevator door.

"Sorry," she said, "Emergency surgery."

The door whooshed shut, leaving a puzzled looking doctor staring after her.

Though Janet had stolen the largest smock she could find in the supply closet, it was still far too small for her. The sleeves reached barely past her elbows, and she'd had to leave it unfastened in front. It was hardly surprising that the doctor had not been altogether convinced of her legitimacy.

Well, she only had to get across one more floor, she told herself, and through the emergency room—and they were always so busy there, it was unlikely anyone would try to stop her. If they did....

"Be brave," she whispered to the unconscious Melissa. "I'll have you out of here soon, where I can take proper care of you. I won't leave you in here, where that evil Wald could find you. He's bound to think of that eventually."

The elevator door opened. Putting her head down again, Janet pushed the bed into the first floor corridor.

The emergency room was as packed and in as much of an uproar as she had predicted. No one even seemed to notice the enormous female doctor in the undersized tunic pushing an unconscious patient out the receiving doors.

90

A pair of medics rushed in with another patient just as she went out. Their ambulance sat empty at the dock, rear doors standing open, motor still running.

Janet wheeled the bed into the rear of the vehicle, fastened it down and closed the doors.

Inside the emergency room, EMT Luis Cordero heard the slam of a door and, curious, glanced through the glass doors to the arrival dock. To his disbelief, he saw someone jump behind the wheel of his ambulance and a moment later the vehicle began to back around.

"Hey, stop" he shouted, running toward the doors, "You can't take that," but he was too late. Even as he pushed through the doors, the ambulance jumped forward with a squeal of tires on pavement and careened down the drive at breakneck speed, almost colliding with another arriving ambulance.

* * * * * * *

Melissa Hyde was gone, vanished from her hospital room.

Curly had been given the job of watching her until she regained consciousness. Sylvester had ordered him to change into jeans and a body-builder tee shirt for the assignment.

"But I won't look like a real agent," Curly had objected. He had only recently been ordained a real agent and he was inordinately proud of the regulation dark suit and what it symbolized. He was an American, a patriot, a part of the team, defending his country from evil. The way he saw it, you could not look like a true defender of the American way in jeans and a body shirt.

"You will look like a bodyguard," Sylvester answered when he voiced his objection. "Which is what you will be."

Curly did not even clearly understand why he was supposed to be guarding this dame. In his opinion, what they needed was to see that she stayed quiet permanently, and the best time to do that was while she was out cold. That way she couldn't scream or put up a struggle. He might not be as smart as Sylvester, but he knew that much at least about defending the American way.

Sylvester had been very definite about wanting the woman alive, however. "See that no one else gets close to her," he ordered, "Except for the doctors and the nurses, and you stick around whenever they are with her. And the minute she starts to come around, you phone me."

The problem was, there was no one now to stick to. She wasn't there. And the nurse on duty had no explanation to offer for the disappearance. She did not even want to go close to the room to see for herself, let alone into it.

All she could say was that there had been an intruder in bed with the patient, but when Curly checked, there was no sign of anyone, only a lingering smell reminiscent of wet hair, and a bedpan and a pee stain where someone had apparently dumped the bedpan on the floor.

Looking at the stain left by the puddle, he could not help but think that they were sure lackadaisical about bathroom cleanliness in this hospital. Whenever he got pee on the floor at home—and gosh, it was just one of those things that happened to everybody sometimes, wasn't it—he always cleaned it up first thing, especially if it was a big puddle, like this one obviously had been. A few drops, okay, he could see leaving that where it was, as long as it didn't stain the rug or get in your food, but a big puddle like this, in a hospital? *Jeez?*

"She was there, I tell you," Nurse Kravitz insisted. "The patient, and there was another woman with her."

Curly checked the notes Sylvester had given him. "Was the other one a skinny broad, about five foot five inches, hair....?" He read aloud from the description.

"No," Nurse Kravitz interrupted sharply.

"No hair?" That was great news, the way he saw it. A bald woman would be easy to spot, since most of them had hair.

"No, I mean she was big," Nurse Kravitz said. "She was enormous. Seven-foot-tall at least, eight-foot. I don't know, maybe nine-foot, even."

Curly looked at his notes again and shook his head. He had been instructed especially to watch out for this Janet Jackle broad and if she showed up to take her into custody. Obviously this couldn't be her, though, not at seven or eight or nine feet tall. His notes clearly said five foot five inches. So that must have been somebody else, for sure.

"Probably this was just some crazy," he said, "I bet she was a homeless person looking for a place to sack out. A wino, maybe, there's a lot of them on the streets these days. That's one of the things that Homeland Security is working to change, to make people's lives safer from winos."

"She threatened me," Nurse Kravitz said with a sob, burying her face in her hands. Her shoulders shook convulsively.

Head Nurse Corinne Dickson, who was trying to make sense of the story and to placate an obviously hysterical Nurse Kravitz, said in a calming voice, "She threatened to harm you?"

"She threatened me with her pussy."

Curly looked dumbfounded. He had trouble processing that bit of information. Nurse Dickson, who was known throughout the hospital for her unflappable professionalism, gave him an embarrassed look over the head of the weeping Gladys Kravitz's.

"There now, Nurse Kravitz," Nurse Dickson began in her most soothing voice.

"It snarled at me," Nurse Kravitz cried, refusing to be mollified. "Her pussy. It crept across the room toward me and it snarled." She did a hoarse imitation of a snarl that sounded more like she was clearing an asthmatic throat.

"Nurse Kravitz has been working double shifts," Nurse Dickson told Curly in an apologetic voice. "It's a very stressful job."

Curly nodded. He had always thought pussies were mysterious things, having had no real experience of them except for that naughty coloring book Lawrence had given him and in which he was looking forward to coloring the pictures, and he had only the vaguest idea of what they might or might not be able to do. He had a difficult time, however, picturing one creeping across the floor, and he was almost certain that snarling was not a usual part of their repertoire.

"And she recited, 'Oh, beautiful pussy, oh pussy my love, what a beautiful pussy you are, you are'." Nurse

Kravitz looked up at Curly through tear-flecked lashes. "The Owl and the Pussycat."

"Jesus! There was an owl too?" Curly farted in trumpet tones.

"I'm not making this up," Nurse Kravitz wailed.

* * * * * * *

"I'm absolutely sure that it was this Drag Thing Jake and I saw, dancing down the street," Teri said. "And I have to say, she was truly a sight. You couldn't help but laugh."

Teri lay sprawled across the bed, basking in the afterglow of a particularly erotic session of lovemaking. She had hardly been able to wait to get home, to her Peter.

"Unfortunately," she added more soberly, "The reality is, Drag Thing is not really a laughing matter. When she starts mugging people, she is no longer a joke. Then she becomes a menace to society. And the menace must be removed."

"That man is lying," Peter said. A cloud of steam trailed his words from the bathroom.

"What makes you say that?"

"He was the one slapping the woman around," Peter said.

"Peter, you weren't even there when it happened, how could you possibly know that?" Teri asked.

The toilet flushed loudly. Peter appeared in the bathroom door, naked save for a damp towel draped over his shoulder. She gave him an approving look. She dearly did love his slim, sculptured body, like a swimmer's or a gymnast's. So many men had to work hard to keep that look, but with Peter it all came naturally.

She also sorely envied him. For her, it was an hour at the gym three times a week, and a good three-mile run every other day. He never even had to break a sweat.

"Caleb Wald, isn't that who you said it was? Of Wald-Med Pharmaceuticals, right? Where I work nights, if you'll recall." He had not told her yet that he had been fired. At least, he thought he had been fired, though it was not altogether clear to him.

"You mean you know him?" Teri asked.

"Not exactly," he said, "Not on a personal level. But let's say I hear rumors. People talk."

"But there were witnesses to the assault," she said.

"Witnesses can lie, too, you know." He tossed the towel aside and began to dress.

"It's funny you should say that," she said, her thoughts turning again to the mystery of Drag Thing, of who she was and where she had come from. "I felt the same thing myself. I was convinced that Caleb Wald was lying when I talked to him, and that Janet Jackle person certainly seemed to think he was. I thought so at first, anyway, until the man in the dark suit spoke up. He's the one who said that Drag Thing...."

"There wasn't anybody else there at the time Wald was slapping the woman around," Peter said adamantly.

"You keep talking as if you were there."

"It's just...well, it's just my intuition, is all," he said.

"Yes, well, unfortunately, honey, intuition weighs less than eyewitness accounts. I just wish I had gotten their statements."

"Exactly."

He pulled jeans up over narrow hips and fastened them. Watching him, it occurred to her, not for the first time, that he looked a little peaked. "Are you feeling all right?" she asked, concerned.

"I think I picked up a little dose of something when I wasn't careful."

"You need to take better care of yourself, Bunny. Maybe you should take the night off," she said. "Maybe we should both take the night off, now that I think of it. I'll stay home, too, and spoon-feed you chicken soup. There's a can in the cupboard."

"No," he said quickly. "I mean, there's no one else to call at this late hour, to take my shift. I'll be okay, don't worry yourself." He was afraid of what was happening to him, afraid it might happen right in front of Teri. Whatever it was, he added. He still couldn't fathom it. But he felt pretty sure he didn't want Teri to see it.

"Okay. You're the boss." She got up from the bed and went to the big oak armoire where she kept her uniforms. To her surprise, the door would not open. She tugged at it again, and realized that the key was missing from the lock, where they usually left it. "Why is this locked?" she asked.

"I...." He hesitated. "I moved your uniforms to the closet there," he said finally.

"But why? What's in here that's so special I can't see it?"

"Christmas is coming," he said after only the briefest of pauses.

"Oh." She gave him an uncertain look and started for the bathroom, but at the door she turned back to look worriedly at him. "Peter, you would tell me, wouldn't you, if there were something wrong?" she said.

"Wrong? What way, wrong?" he asked innocently.

"Well, you know, with us, I guess is what I'm trying to say." She smiled a bit timidly.

"Absolutely, there is nothing wrong between the two of us." He said it with such sincerity that Teri could not possibly disbelieve him. She smiled again, more genuinely this time, and blew him a kiss.

"One thing that really puzzles me about this whole Drag Thing business," she said from the bathroom, "is how he and I keep crossing paths. It's as if something is drawing us together, as if there were some kind of bond between us. That's silly, isn't it? What connection could there possibly be between me and Drag Thing?" Without waiting for an answer, she started the shower.

The moment he heard the water running, Peter went to the dresser for his keys. *Did I lock the armoire,* he asked himself? Yes, he must have: there on his ring was the key that was normally just left in the door of the armoire. They had never had any reason to lock it. Even before he opened the armoire doors, however, he had a sinking expectation of what he would find.

It was just as he had feared: the armoire was filled with dresses. There was the blue one from before and a new one the color of fresh butter. He recognized that fabric, too. He had specifically selected it for an outfit for Teri. It really had

96

been intended for a Christmas present, but this dress certainly would not do for her, not with her exquisite figure. This was the size of a circus tent.

He put his hands on his temples and squeezed hard. Nothing made sense any more. He thought of those dreams he had been having lately. They seemed so real that part of him had to believe they actually were happening to him, that he really had been there the night before when Caleb Wald had struck the woman in the alley. How could he have dreamed something that really happened?

A thought suddenly occurred to him: no, that could *not* have been him, not wearing either of these dresses. He took the blue one from the closet. Since he had last seen it, someone had added enormous ruffles at the neck and the sleeves and a sunburst of sequins on the bodice. It was incredibly vulgar.

More to the point, though, it was incredibly large, oceans too large for him. When he held it up in front of him the hem trailed across the floor. Grimalkin strolled up and sniffed disdainfully at it.

No, whatever the explanation was, he could not have worn this dress. He would have tripped over himself just trying to walk in it. This looked as if it had been made for someone eight feet tall.

"What does it all mean?" he asked the cat. Could someone else be sneaking in here and dressing up, and using his fabrics and sewing machine to whip up costumes? Surely that made even less sense than supposing he had been cavorting on the streets in one of these outfits—which was equally ridiculous.

The shower ended in the bathroom. He quickly closed the armoire, locked it again, and pocketed the keys. He would think about it all later, when Teri was gone. Right now, what he needed more than anything else was sleep. He felt like shit—as if he had been up all night.

CHAPTER EIGHT

"Whoa, you look like shit."

Peter rubbed the sleep from his eyes and squinted at their downstairs neighbor, Lee Appel—known affectionately to his friends as Lorelie Lee.

"Thanks, I love you too," Peter said, yawning. "What's up?"

"Well, I thought you were. I heard all this galumphing around up here, so I brought you some of my come-again-on-the-tapioca cake, a generous slice of which I will trade for a cuppa. What's this?"

He swished past Peter and snatched up the yellow dress from the floor. "Mother of Pearl, would you look at the size of this! I know it's Halloween, but what were you going as, a Peterbilt in drag?"

"It's for a large woman," Peter said.

"A large woman? Honey I could get in here with two of my sisters and still have room for bumpies."

"Bumpies?"

That earned him a withering look "Bumping genitals together, to put it in delicate words. It's what two girls do in bed. Or two Nellie queens. Sweetie, this could not be for the lovely Teri. Don't tell me you've got a circus job."

Peter sighed. "What I have got is a problem," he said. He hesitated, embarrassed to try to explain. But he had to unburden himself to someone, didn't he? His head was practically bursting with everything banging around inside it. And in a sense, this was Lee's kind of thing. He dressed in drag all the time. He was wearing a lavender peignoir just at the moment. Who better than him to understand; or, if not understand, at least to offer a sympathetic ear?

"Come on, let's get that coffee brewing," he said. "I need to talk."

"And aside from tush, waistline and bust, I am practically nothing but ears," Lee said, following him into the kitchen and savoring, as he always did, the curves of his friend's shapely bottom.

He sighed wistfully, but with no real hope. *If only....*

* * * * * * *

Peter told it all, from the vial and the syringe left in the lab and his accidentally pricking himself, and that strange cat in the cage, to the street punks, the Moes; from the stash of makeup he had "purchased" at For The Girls, to The Copa Club and the run-in with Caleb Wald, and the destruction at the lab and those men who had accosted him there.

"And then there's the dresses," he concluded. "The one in there, and there is another one in the armoire, and for all I know, a new one on the sewing machine, and it must be me who's making them, it sure isn't Grimalkin. And on top of everything else, I am out of a job. How am I going to explain that to Teri? How am I going to explain any of it?"

Lee had sat in silence throughout the story, nodding his head occasionally or pursing his lips. Now he sighed loudly. "Are you pulling my leg or is my garter too tight?" he asked when Peter had finished.

"Does that sound like something I could make up?" Peter asked.

"No. No, I suppose not," Lee agreed. "You are creative, sugar, but not that creative. Anyway, I think I remember, there was something in the paper this morning, about that business outside The Copa."

"There was? What did it say?" Peter asked, excited.

"I don't remember exactly, I didn't pay much attention. I was looking for Macy's sale ads. Let me go get the paper." Lee pushed the plate with the coffee cake toward Peter. "Eat, keep up your strength," he said, "I'll be right back."

He returned in a few minutes, carrying a folded newspaper. "I thought I remembered this," he said, sitting back down at the kitchen table. "Here it is, on page two. I didn't think much of it when I read it. I mean, other people attack drag queens so often, I just thought it was sauce for the gander when I read it. 'Drag Queen Assaults Couple'," he read aloud. "'Victim says man in drag looked like Godzilla in a cheap blue dress'."

"Cheap?" Peter exploded. "That fabric cost thirty-nine ninety five a yard, and that was on sale. Regular price was…."

"The interesting thing is," Lee said, "They make this Drag Thing out to be the villain, like he was the assailant, and not the way you told it."

"I will admit, the sequins do cheapen it somewhat," Peter said, "But the ruffles add a little…."

"Get a grip would you?" Lee snapped. "There is something more important here than a dress" He rolled his eyes and slapped himself on the cheek. "Merciful Minerva," he gasped, "Who would ever have thought to hear those shallow words coming from my mouth?"

He gave Peter a speculative look. "I don't suppose you would want to say Shazzam or whatever it is you do to turn into this Franken-drag? I would sort of like to see her for myself."

"But I don't know how to do it. It just happens on its own, I think," Peter said.

"Hmm. I'll bet it would scare the pee out of the ladies at the hospital tearoom if you went off at the wrong time. Though to be frank some of those girls would be happy to have a man go off at any time and in any fashion."

"I'm scared, Lee," Peter said earnestly. "Am I going to remain this…this Alley Thing forever?"

"Well, it doesn't seem like a real tragedy, if you ask me. It just means you've got a secret life."

"Not a very nice one," Peter said.

"That is part of the fun of having a secret life, sugar. Anyway, If you want my opinion, we are all of us alley things, some of us just clean up better than others. What I do not get here is, why the drag routine? I mean, why *you* in drag?" He tossed the newspaper aside and gave Peter a long, measuring look. "Okay, now, tell the truth and shame the devil, sweetie, is this something you have pondered before? Putting on a dress, I mean?"

"Well, I kind of...." Peter stammered and turned red.

"I thought so," Lee said with a nod of his head. "To be perfectly frank, I sort of sometimes wondered, well, you know, with the dresses and all. I mean, it's not exactly he-man stuff, is it?"

"I am not gay, Lee, I swear I'm not, I'd tell you if I were," Peter said. "It's just that dresses, and women's things, they, they fascinate me, they always have, even when I was a little boy. I used to pore over my mother's fashion magazines the way some boys read car magazines. But except for a frilly little apron and some of Teri's Chanel Number Five, I have never put anything on before, really. It's just something I have dreamed about for years. I was afraid if I told anyone, they would think, well, you know."

"That you were gay?" Lee finished for him. "Pish posh. Drag and gay are not the same thing at all. You would be surprised how many men I have known who wear silk panties under their jeans. Real men, I'm talking here, boots and construction helmets, all the butch stuff. The tranny world—that's transgender to you—comes in all sizes and colors and flavors, and every conceivable sexual orientation. Trans-sexuals, drag queens, drag kings...."

"Drag kings?" Peter said, puzzled.

"That's women who dress up as men. You really are an innocent, aren't you? I can see we are going to have to do some educating. But the point I was getting at is, maybe this stuff, whatever it was, this Alley Thing business, maybe it does not altogether change a person. Maybe it just takes what is already in there, so to speak, and, like, blows it up, in a manner of speaking. You secretly wanted to put on a dress, you accidentally get a shot of this stuff, whatever in Heaven's name it is, and poof, you are a Drag Thing. If you were into hairy guys, you might have turned into a Teddy bear."

"You may be right, but I don't see how that is going to help me," Peter said with a sigh. "Golly, things couldn't possibly get any worse for me, could they?"

"Oh, honey, things can always get worse, trust me." Peter looked so utterly crestfallen, though, that Lee relented a little. "Look, since you have asked for my advice, I would say the very first thing we have got to do is find those two women doctors and tell them what has happened. They are the ones who brewed this up, aren't they? They should either fix it or bottle it, in which case I am making a mental list of people I could spoon it to. I mean, think what it could do to someone who is secretly a sex maniac. I have this one trick…well, never mind, that's a different story. Do you have any ideas where to start looking for these women?"

"One of them was in a coma," Peter said. "They took her to a hospital. Saint Maria Alfonso's, I think it was."

"Well, that rules her out, at least until she comes around, if she does. And that could be years, knowing that hospital. What about the other one?"

Peter shrugged. "I don't have a clue where she could be. It must have been her who demolished the lab, mustn't it? And Wald and those men with him were looking for her, I'm pretty sure. Although judging from the condition in which she left the lab, I feel pretty sure she will not want to be found."

"It doesn't sound like she is going to be having us over for tea, then. So we will have to go looking for her." Lee thought for a moment. "Well, silly me, I'm not thinking straight," he said, brightening, "It is the High Holy Days."

"The what?"

"The Bitch's Sabbath." When Peter continued to look confused, he said peevishly, "Halloween. Tomorrow. Honestly, you butch ones. I'll bet you chop logs to make your own toothpicks."

"Okay, so it's Halloween. So what?" Peter asked.

"So what? So, the Castro is ground zero for Halloween celebration. If there is anywhere public that dyke is likely to show up, that would be the spot."

"With everything that has happened, do you really think she would be out celebrating?" Peter asked doubtfully.

"It is not about celebrating, sugar, it is practically required of our people," Lee said, "It's called showing the flag.

Lesbians get a frequent flyer mile for every minute they spend in the Castro on Halloween night."

"What about gay men?"

"A mile and a half. It's those eyelashes, they are a bitch to get right, lots harder than putting on a leather jacket." Lee stood up and dusted his hands together. "That's it, then. You get yourself gussied up and I will pick you up tomorrow night at nine. We are going to do the Stro, sweets, the two of us. And you had better look fabulous, too. I want all those ladies to be so-o-o jealous when they see you with me."

"I don't know," Peter said hesitantly.

"The macho look." Lee looked Peter up and down. "You do do macho, don't you? It isn't all dresses, I hope."

Peter laughed despite himself. He was glad now that he had told Lee everything. Even if Lee couldn't help him, it was a relief just to share the burden. "I will be so macho it will make you swoon," he promised.

Lee rolled his eyes. "Don't get too carried away, honey, you might end up with me weak and helpless in your arms, and if you think you have got trouble now, you really do not want to go there."

* * * * * * *

"Moes. Check it out." Hector paused to read a hand-lettered sign on a telephone pole, his lips moving as he scanned. "Someone's offering a reward for his lost doggie. Fifty frigging bucks. Man. We could make ourselves some easy cash."

The other two glanced at the poster. Archie shrugged. "So? We don't have his little doggie, do we?"

"No, but we could have," Hector said. "Not his little doggie, exactly, but, you know, we could have someone's little doggie. People love their doggies. Fags especially. They totally freak out over their doggies. I'll bet they offer rewards all the time when their doggies get lost."

He gave them a minute to catch on. When they still looked at him blankly, he explained patiently, "Say, like, we snatch someone's doggie, some fag's, and we hold him for ransom."

103

"That's a federal case, isn't it, kidnapping?" Tom asked. "I don't want the F.B.I. on my butt, bro. Remember that movie, *The Unstoppables*? That Connery dude? Man, those guys don't quit till they bust your ass. They finally got this big time gangster cause he paid his income tax."

"That's if it's people, dummy," Hector said. "No one cares if you snatch a dog. Except the dog's fag owner. And what if they busted us anyway? There's no proof the dog didn't just jump into our arms. The dog can't squeal, can he? And as long as we don't pay any income tax that Connery dude can't touch us either, right? We just wait for the fag to offer a reward for his missing doggie, and then we call and say we *found* his pooch roaming the streets, and he can have him back and we collect the reward. I'm telling you, it's easy money, no risks."

Archie grinned. "Rad. Sounds like a plan to me."

"Only," Tom said, "We haven't got a dog."

"Man, that's a bummer," Archie said, his grin fading.

"So? We just go looking for one," Hector said patiently.

"Where?" Tom asked.

"Like, in the Castro, where else?" Hector said. "We want a fag's dog, right? They're the ones that'll pay the big ass bucks. And where do all the fags live? They live in the Castro. So, that's where we look for a doggie."

"Sweet. You are sharp, bro, you know that?" Archie said with an admiring grin.

"I love this town," Tom said. "It's got everything a dude could want—fags, doggies, all of it. Hyuk, hyuk, hyuk."

"Only, the Castro's a long way from here. I can't stroll that far with this," Archie said, indicating the crutch he had stolen a little earlier from the vestibule of a senior center. His leg was better, but it still hurt to walk on it.

"*No problema*," Hector said, "I saw a little gray Toyota sitting at the curb a couple of blocks back there practically inviting someone to go for a cruise of the Castro. All we got to do is a little specialty wiring...."

"I can do that," Archie said.

They went back to the little gray Toyota. The owner had left the doors conveniently unlocked. Archie sprawled on the front seat and began tugging at electrical wires underneath the dash. Sparks flared.

"Whoa," Tom declared, watching with rapt interest.

"Got her," Archie said. The engine turned over a bit reluctantly, and came to life. Within five minutes they were on their way to the Castro, Archie at the wheel, Hector beside him and Tom in the back

"This is even better," Hector said, picking something up from the seat between them. "Check it out, bros, the dude left his cell phone. We can call people all over the place."

He played with the phone and contemplated whom he might call. Unfortunately, almost no one he knew had a phone and the ones who did wouldn't be interested in hearing from him. He punched in numbers at random and got a woman's voice: "Lydia's Lace-aria, where the ladies of the street meet, Maggie the manager speaking. Can I help you with your intimate undies?"

"You got Prince Albert on the can?" Hector asked and hung up laughing.

"What's that mean?" Archie asked, frowning. "Exactly?"

Hector shrugged. *Fucking boneheads spoiled everything.* "I don't know. Some chick I used to know called people all the time and asked that, and then she'd hang up and she'd just about pee her pants laughing."

"It's probably some in joke," Tom said. "Hyuk, hyuk, hyuk."

"Yeah, gotta be. Take the side streets," Hector instructed.

"Dude, we just lifted the car five, ten minutes ago, the cops won't be looking for it yet," Archie said. "Probably the dude hasn't even missed it."

Hector sighed. Sometimes these two tried his patience. It was just lucky for them that he, at least, had brains. "We're looking for doggies," he explained with exaggerated care. "Unattended doggies. We want residential streets, not queenie shops like on Market Street." He paused thoughtfully. "What do you think a lace-aria is? What are intimate undies, anyway?"

Drag Thing, by Victor J. Banis

* * * * * * *

It took fewer than ten minutes for them to find the dog they wanted, at the edge of the Castro on a street where most of the silent houses, windows dark, looked already settled in for the night.

They found several dogs, in fact. A small pack of them was clustered outside a big iron fence, one of them trying in vain to dig a hole under the fence in the cement of the sidewalk.

Archie pulled up to the curb and the Moes got out. The dogs looked at them eagerly as if they were reinforcements. The digger stopped and waited.

"Check it out, there must be a dozen of them. We could take them all," Tom said. "Get a whole bunch of rewards."

"Numb nuts," Hector said, giving him a swat on the back of his head. "These mutts are running loose. Nobody cares enough about them to pay us anything. That's the one we want, the doggie in the window." Hector jerked a thumb beyond the iron fence. A lone pug sat in the window, panting and staring longingly at the dog pack outside the fence.

"How much could we get for the doggie in the window, do you think?" Archie asked.

"A C note, for sure," Hector said.

"No way," Archie said, disbelieving.

"Way," Hector insisted. "I'm telling you, a C note."

"Look, ain't that cute, he's wearing panties," Tom said. He frowned thoughtfully. "Only, why would a dog wear panties, you think?"

"Because he's special," Hector explained. *Jeez, these two dipshits.* "I told you, fruits are really weird about their little dogs, they treat them like they were their babies. That tells us this one is something totally special to his owner. A guy who puts little pink panties on his dog, he probably walks him in a baby buggy too. For sure he will pay a reward. Big time. C note, for sure. All we got to do now is snatch the pup."

Archie and Tom exchanged glances. "I can't get over the fence with this," Archie said, indicting the crutch. Tom looked at Hector.

106

"I got to keep an eye out," Hector said. "I'm the one working the plan, right? Besides...." He indicated the make-shift sling on his arm and looked at Tom. "You'll have to climb over."

Tom looked briefly doubtful but as usual he couldn't think of any good argument for Hector's superior reasoning. With a put-upon sigh he turned to the iron spikes.

He managed to clamber over the fence with only one small tear in his jeans, and dropped to the ground on the other side with a loud "Woof." The pack of dogs on the sidewalk danced about noisily and watched his every move intently, as if wanting to hitch a ride.

"Now what?" Tom asked, standing and dusting himself off.

"Duh. Now you get Fido," Hector said. "That's what you climbed over there for, isn't it?"

Tom stared at the doggie in the window for a moment. The pug stared back, tongue lolling, and wagged her tail, her entire rear wagging with it. "The window's shut," Tom said, looking back at Hector. "How do I get it open?"

Jesus, I got to think of everything, Hector thought wea-rily. "See if there's a screwdriver in the car," he told Archie. "Or a tire iron, maybe. Something he can get the window open with."

Archie checked the trunk of the car and was back a min-ute later with a foot long screwdriver. "Here you go," he said, handing it to Hector.

"It's for him, not me," Hector said, pointing a thumb at Tom. *Talk about stupid.*

Archie handed the screwdriver through the fence. Tom took it from him and went to the window, and holding the screwdriver by the blade, he smashed the glass with the han-dle. Hector sighed and poised to run in case the noise brought an angry resident, but for the moment there was no response from inside.

"Get the fuckin' window open," he hissed loudly.

Tom lifted the sash up. "Shit, it wasn't locked to begin with," he said, looking over his shoulder with a sheepish grin.

"Get the damned dog, then, and let's go," Hector said. *Man, these guys could drive you fucking around the bend.*

Tom reached through the broken glass and picked up the pug. The dogs on the sidewalk wagged their tails in celebration and pranced about excitedly, their toenails clicking on the pavement. There was a chorus of eager yips and arfs and wheezes.

"Give him to me," Hector said. Tom handed the pug over the fence. "Come on." Hector said to Archie, "We need to make a quick getaway before someone comes to investigate. Neighbors are probably calling the cops already, dumb fuck breaking the window like that."

"Hey, what about me?" Tom demanded, scrabbling up the iron fence.

"Ought to leave him here, dude ran out on us the other night," Hector said under his breath. "Hey, get off." The pack of dogs was jumping at his legs, trying to get at the pug. They almost tripped him up. "Fuck, dumb dogs. Go away. Fuck off. Shit, what's with these little bastards anyway, I never saw dogs so excited?"

Archie had the car door open. Hector threw the pug onto the back seat and slid in after him. He had to kick two of the most aggressive dogs away to keep them from jumping in as well. One of them got past and managed to get inside. Hector picked him up and tossed him at the others. "Haul ass, bro," he told Archie.

"Hey, bros," Tom yelled. He fell over the fence and landed on his hands and knees on the sidewalk among the frantic dogs. He just made it into the car as it started to move. "Fuck, you guys almost left me behind," he said, flinging himself into the back seat and panting.

"No shit," Hector said.

"Man, that was one friendly bunch of dogs, wasn't it?" Archie said with a laugh. "Guess this little dude must be one of their bros. I'll bet they're Moe dogs."

"I'll bet it's them little pink panties he's wearing that got them all excited," Tom said.

"I'll bet them little pink panties got you all excited," Hector said.

108

"Gee, I don't know." Tom gave the pug a measuring look. "I remember once when I was a kid, we had this big old hound dog, his name was Fred, and this one time I...."

"Forget it," Hector said, pretty sure he didn't want to hear the rest. "This here is our meal ticket."

"Speaking of meals...," Archie said. It had been a long time since they had last eaten.

"Yeah, we got to make a grocery run," Hector said. "Head for Safeway."

* * * * * * *

They made a food foray through the Safeway supermarket, each picking up something for supper. Hector was tempted by a fragrant roast chicken, still warm from the oven, but he figured the smell would tip off the security guard by the door. Steaks were better because you couldn't smell them if a guy walked out with them, but they had no way of cooking them back at the Bat Cave.

Instead, he slipped a package of doughnuts under his parka, the glazed kind. Doughnuts were always good for a meal. And some ice cream, too, a quart of vanilla and a quart of chocolate. Ice cream was great with doughnuts. He went back and got a box of chocolate doughnuts as well, for dessert.

He had been thinking lately that maybe he would split for a while. Head for Las Vegas, say. He bet he could show those show girls a thing or two. Or someplace foreign, but where they spoke American. Hawaii, maybe, or that Gilligan's Island. He had seen that once on TV and it looked totally cool. Especially that blonde babe. He was willing to bet she'd dig his coconuts.

A chick stacking cans of vegetables on a shelf gave him the eye. He winked at her as he went by and strutted a little more confidently. When he was by himself, he would get a lot more pussy, too, he was convinced of it. Those two shit heads he was hanging out with, you could count on them to scare a chick away. No wonder he was spending all his time whacking off instead of getting laid right, like he was sure he could if he was on his own.

Maybe, he thought, his stomach reminding him he was hungry, maybe he could stash the chocolate doughnuts and have them all for himself when the boneheads were asleep. And the ice cream too, at least the chocolate.

The other two were already at the car when he got back to it. Tom had gotten chips and cheese puffs, which didn't seem to Hector like he had picked up his fair share. Man, sometimes he thought he was the only one could do things right. Maybe it *was* time for him to move on.

"Sardines," Archie said, brandishing cans. "And pork and beans. And, check this out." He produced a large bag of M&Ms with a flourish.

"Wow, dudes, this is gonna be like a banquet," Tom said. "Hyuk, hyuk, hyuk." He glanced at the car. The pug was jumping at the window, little nails making clickety-click sounds on the glass. "Uh oh. We forgot about Fido."

"So? We ain't running a doggie camp," Hector said. "The dog'll live till tomorrow."

"No way. I ain't letting the pup go hungry," Tom said stubbornly. "That's not cool."

"So, what? You want to go back in?" Hector asked.

"Cousin of mine has dogs," Archie said, "And she feeds them, like, people stuff all the time. You know, leftovers."

"Okay, fine," Hector said. "The doggie can eat what we eat, nothing wrong with that, way I see it. Good thing I got plenty, though." *I definitely am gonna stash the ice cream,* he thought. For sure he was doing more than his fair share.

A pair of dogs bounded across the parking lot toward them, barking merrily. One of them tried to climb Hector's leg. "Get off," he said, shaking the dog loose. "The hounds must have smelled the ice cream."

Another dog joined the two dancing around their feet. Hector kicked at him. "Shit, what's with all the dogs?" he demanded. "Don't the city have a dogcatcher? Fucker's not doing his job, don't seem like to me."

"Maybe you oughta write somebody a letter," Tom said.

"Yeah, I got a good mind," Hector said. He didn't bother to explain that he could barely write. All those words, it was hard to fit them together. Thinking was what he did best anyway. "Let's head for the Bat Cave."

CHAPTER NINE

The Bat Cave was just the top floor in an abandoned house at the edge of the Mission. Other homeless and drifters came and went, but the Moes had made it clear to one and all that the top floor was their turf exclusively and woe to anyone who forgot it. Almost nobody ever did, in part because many of the buildings other residents were in no condition most of the time to manage the rickety stairs to get there. Even the rats that ran freely on the other floors, and the cats that came looking for them, shunned the top one.

There was a sleeping bag on the floor that they had stolen off of a bicycle a while back and a torn mattress that had been left out on the sidewalk for the trash collectors and except for some mildew and a spring that poked out at one end, was perfectly fine for sleeping on.

They had a trio of DVDs, ripped off from a parked car and which they hadn't yet seen because they had neither a player nor a TV: *Seven Brides for Seven Brothers* (from the title they thought that might be a porno flick), *The Opening of Misty Beethoven* (which they were almost sure was porn), and *The Terminator* (which Archie had seen years before and confidently proclaimed "the baddest movie ever").

There were lots of comic books scattered on the floor—mostly *X-Men* and *Spider Man*—and a generous selection of well-thumbed *Playboy*s and *Hustler*s salvaged from recycling bins ("Can you believe it, some jerk-off would throw these away?").

They had been crashing at the Bat Cave now for better than two months, and it had begun to seem like home to them. They no longer even noticed the stench of urine and rotted garbage nor the mildew on the mattress. Before the

Bat Cave they had been sleeping on sidewalks and in doorways or on the grass in Dolores Park, so this was definitely a step up for them. It had been a long time since any of them had known a better home.

Hector managed to hide the chocolate doughnuts behind a box. The ice cream had mostly melted by now, though, so he didn't bother trying to stash that. They passed around the cartons and spooned some on to the floor for the pug. Chips and cheese puffs went around, and sardines and pork and beans, and the M&Ms. They had lifted a case of beer from an unwatched delivery truck on the way home and they belched and toasted one another enthusiastically with warm beer as they ate. The pug welcomed all and even enthusiastically lapped up some beer, which earned the Moe's hearty approval.

"All right," Archie said, beaming approval. "We got ourselves a party dog."

The only sour spot was that a stray mutt got into the house somehow and tried to crash the party. They shoved him out and closed the door to their room. For a while they could hear him outside whining and occasionally barking, and scratching at the door, but by the time they had finished most of the beer, he had ceased to whine or bark, although he still scratched from time to time. By then, the Moes were all asleep.

The pug sat at the closed door for a long while, listening to the dog on the other side sniff and scratch, and occasionally glancing back at the sleeping trio.

After a time, she went into a far corner and scented around until she found a spot to do her business. She came back and curled up on the mattress next to Tom. He put an arm around her in his sleep, and she settled closer, and drifted off as well.

* * * * * * *

Sylvester was furious to learn that Melissa Hyde had disappeared from the hospital. "You were supposed to be guarding her," he told Curly.

"I couldn't help it," Curly defended himself. "It happened before I got here."

"Then you should have gotten here sooner," Sylvester said.

"Besides, I don't get it—how could someone just walk off with person in a hospital bed?" Curly said. "I mean, it's not like they could walk out together holding hands or nothing. The one in the coma was unconscious."

"Whoever took her stole an ambulance," Nurse Dickson said. "A very tall, ugly doctor with bright red hair, according to the description. He wheeled her right out the emergency bay and stole an ambulance, and they were gone before anybody could stop them. The police are searching for them, of course. I understand they're stopping every ambulance to look for them. But, there are so many ambulances on the streets of San Francisco. And they do all look alike."

Curly thought that Saint Alfonso's was a pretty sloppily run hospital, what with puddles of pee left on floors, and patients carted away at random and missing ambulances—but he left his thoughts unspoken.

He was in enough trouble as it was.

* * * * * * *

It had been a first for EMT Luis Cordero, losing his ambulance.

"Thirty years, and we've never lost one," his dispatcher said with an angry shake of his head.

"Listen, it wasn't just us," Luis had pointed out. "Don't forget, Saint Maria Alfonso lost a patient."

"Well, that's too bad for them, but they lose patients by the carload, every day of the week at that joint. The difference is, they don't get their paychecks docked, like we probably will. Do you have any idea how much an ambulance costs? You'll be paying forever. We both will. Till we're old, old ladies."

Nevertheless, the emergency workload in San Francisco was too heavy to have a driver just sitting on the bench. An hour later, Luis was on the streets again, in another vehicle—

and none too soon, either. He was barely behind the wheel when he got a call on an emergency appendectomy.

He made it to the scene in no time flat. He had his record to think of. If he got no more demerits, the company might give him a break and write off the missing ambulance. More than that, there was his reputation to consider. Plus, though this was something of an afterthought, occupied as he was with the damage to his work record, but there were the wounded and the sick to consider as well. You couldn't altogether ignore them.

They had barely shoved the patient into the rear of the ambulance before Luis was behind the wheel and they were moving, headed once again for Saint Maria Alfonso.

"Hey, wait a sec," his paramedic shouted. "I haven't even got this guy strapped down yet."

"No time," Luis called back. "You said yourself this one was critical. Just hold on to him, why don't you? It's only a couple of miles. We'll be there before I could stop and help you get him fastened down. Okay?"

"Well, okay, I guess so," was the somewhat reluctant answer. "But step on it, okay?"

"Trust me," Luis said. "You won't know what hit you."

"Please," the patient moaned in a feeble voice. "I'm really…."

"Don't you worry now, sir," Luis called to him, "You're going to get a ride you will never forget."

They had gone no more than a couple of blocks, however, when Luis saw flashing red lights in his mirror and heard the wail of a siren. A police car—his immediate thought was that they must have caught the call on the emergency, and were here to give him an escort.

"All right," he said aloud, grinning broadly, and speeded up. With a squad car clearing the way for him, he'd be at the hospital quicker than ever. A couple of record-time trips and he might even make Employee of the Month. Let them try to fire him then. More than likely, he'd get a raise. For sure a commendation. Everyone would forget all about that missing ambulance. It was just a woman in a coma, after all. Who was she going to complain to? Maybe she hadn't even been kidnapped, maybe she had just run away. That happened

114

sometimes with patients at Saint Maria Alfonso—not that he could blame them, really. He'd heard rumors recently of pee-stains on the floors and bedpans left lying around.

The police car caught up with him and pulled alongside on the left and the officer on the passenger side waved out the window. Luis waved back, encouraged, and shot ahead. The ambulance rocketed around a gaggle of cars. The black and white fell behind, then came alongside again, the officer waving all the more frantically.

"Go to the side," he shouted.

To Luis, with the wind noise and both sirens screaming, it sounded like, "Go for the ride." He laughed with delight and gave the man a thumbs up. "I'm with you, man," he shouted in reply. It was times like this that made it all worthwhile. Plus, there was something to be said for saving lives. Especially if you could have fun doing it.

"What's happening, bro?" the paramedic asked from the rear. The vehicle was bouncing and tilting frenziedly as it whipped around traffic. "You're going awfully fast, aren't you? I'm having a helluva time trying to hang on to this guy."

"Hang on to your jockstrap. We're going to set a new land speed record," Luis called back.

"Uh oh. We'd better. I think we just lost him."

They jounced violently over a railroad crossing, the ambulance airborne for a few seconds before it crashed to the pavement again with a mighty groan.

"Urgh," the patient cried, regaining semi-consciousness.

"That brought him back," the paramedic shouted, "but it's touch and go. Maybe a minute, two, even, but I think that's the max."

"We're almost there," Luis cried. "Hold on to him."

Shots rang out. Holes suddenly appeared in the vehicle's rear doors.

"What's that?" The paramedic, a black man, grew visibly paler. "What's happening, man?" he yelled in a panicked voice.

"I...I think...," Luis said, disbelieving. The black and white pulled alongside once more. This time, the officer on the passenger side had his gun in his hand. He fired again.

"Jeez, they're shooting at us," Luis said.

"Shooting at us?! We've got a dying man back here. This is no time for cowboys and Indians. Wait, I'll bet they're white asses, aren't they, both of them? Man, I hate when those honkie cops start playing that macho shit on us. Can't you explain things to them?"

"How can I explain anything to them at eighty miles an hour?" Luis asked, careening around an old lady in a Ford Taurus. The driver of the car, startled out of her wits, lost control and crashed into a pair of parked vehicles, metal shrieking in agony and sparks flying.

"Stay where you are, ma'am. We'll be back for you in a couple of minutes," Luis shouted out the window at her. That would be another quick trip. That commendation was beginning to look more and more like a sure thing. Except for the pesky guys in the black and white....

The cop started shooting again. It crossed Luis' mind in a flash that maybe these weren't even real cops. In San Francisco people dressed up all the time. And tomorrow night was Halloween. The fact that they were in uniform proved nothing. He knew half a dozen queens who, when they got in uniform, looked more like cops than the real thing. If there was anything gay men understood, it was dressing up.

The fact that they were in a black and white proved nothing either. If they could steal ambulances, who was to say they couldn't steal cop cars, too. Besides, he'd already had one ambulance stolen out from under him this evening. Maybe this was another attempt at a theft, an elaborate scheme to hijack him. Maybe ambulances had become the hot new commodity on the stolen vehicle market. Sure, that was it. Had to be.

"I'll bet those punks think they're taking this baby to their chop shop in the Mission," he muttered to himself. Or it was on its way to Tijuana. And he'd have two of these busses to pay for. He'd be eating canned frijoles for the rest of his life.

"Well, they can just think again, they won't get another one off me," he declared sternly. He wasn't falling for their ruse, however cleverly they had planned it. Faux uniforms and stolen black and whites? What did they think he was, some kind of a Rican dummy?

"No way, José." He gripped the wheel ferociously and leaned over it with a determined set to his chin, his eyes fixed on the street ahead. He'd been driving ambulances for fifteen years. The cop had not been born yet who could out-drive him.

The black and white tried to get in front of him, to cut him off. "Hah!" Luis scoffed. "You'll have to do better than that, Jack Off."

He jerked the wheel violently to the left, and his front bumper caught the squad car, sending it skidding with a squeal of tires on pavement. Watching in the mirror, Luis chortled. Probably they thought he was some kind of sissy. That would show them.

In the lead again, he goosed it, pedal to the metal. Checking the mirror, he saw another set of flashing lights in the distance. They must have called in back up. Man, this was some elaborate set up. Two stolen squads. These guys must want ambulances really bad. Maybe there was some kind of crisis in Mexico. Drugs, he'd bet. Or hookers. Think about it, hookers operating out of ambulances, a portable bordello—it was diabolical. His thoughts drifted. He wondered briefly how that might work in the Castro. Say you had a line up of hotties...it would definitely cut down on commute time...

He made a corner on two wheels, the rear of the ambulance catching a utility pole with a loud crunch of metal and bringing his attention back to the moment. More shots rang out. A crack like a giant spider web appeared in the windshield. They bounced over some more tracks.

"Awk," the patient cried from the rear. "Aieee!"

"Fuck! I'm hit," the paramedic yelled. "They got me, man."

"Hang on," Luis said. "We're almost there."

Another black and white appeared in front of them, sliding into position to block the street. Luis veered to the right, onto the sidewalk by the Safeway market. An Indian woman in a bright green sari stepped in front of him, pushing a grocery cart. She saw the ambulance roaring toward her and leaped out of its path with a terrified cry, but he caught the cart. Eggs and milk and something else he couldn't identify splattered across the windshield, practically blinding him. He hit a fence and roared across someone's yard, the ambulance's rear end yawing on wet grass, hit a culvert and went aloft, sailing across a drainage ditch. A snippet of green fabric trailed behind it, flapping like a pennant in their wake.

The patient screamed from the rear. "Help! Help! Someone, help!"

"Be quiet back there," Luis snapped. "Like, I've got my hands full up here. Try thinking about somebody beside yourself for a second, why don't you, fella? Can't you see I need to concentrate?"

He turned on the windshield wipers. The eggs and milk became an omelet. He was flying totally blind now. Something crunched beneath the front wheels—a bicycle, he thought. He hoped there was no one on it.

"*Gran Díos*, save me, save me," the patient cried.

"Shit, save your own ass, dammit," the medic answered. "I'm gone, bro." He threw open the rear door and as the vehicle slowed for a moment to make a tight right turn, he dived through it. The stretcher had only been half fastened, however, and the violent bouncing and swaying had broken it loose altogether. With one last agonized shriek, the patient flew out the flailing door after the paramedic.

Rose Taylor and Estelle Marmachuck were strolling home from grocery shopping, arms linked, chatting about grandchildren and vacation plans, when an ambulance roared past them at breakneck speed.

"What on earth?" Rose cried, but before Estelle could reply, a black man flew out the rear door of the vehicle, arms waving, and landed atop them, knocking all three to the ground—luckily for them, as Rose pointed out subsequently: only seconds later, an airborne stretcher sailed over their heads and landed beyond them in some bushes with a crunch and a horrible wail of anguish.

"We might have been decapitated by that man in the bed," Rose said. "Very thoughtless of him, if you ask me."

"It was like that movie, *The Night of the Living Dead,*" Estelle told the police later. "Bodies flying through the air. It was so exciting."

"Only, I lost my milk," Rose said.

In the ambulance, Luis heard a final shriek quickly dying away. "That's better," he said, as the ambulance got suddenly quieter. "Thank you both."

He tried the windshield washers. He must be close to Saint María Alfonso's by now—if only he could see....

* * * * * * *

The three security agents moved into the Wald-Med Building the same evening, to Caleb's chagrin. Even his displeasure at their presence, however, could not dampen Caleb's excitement over the idea that had come to him in the interim. He could hardly wait to share it with them.

"The Castro," he announced without preamble. The trio looked at him in surprise and puzzlement.

"You mean, like the terrorist in Cuba?" Lawrence asked. "Homeland Security is looking at him. We're monitoring his email. There's this outrageous queen in Miami, Flora Dora the Cuba Libra she calls herself, they write back and forth every day, you should read some of this stuff, talk about hot. I never even thought about what you could do with a beard...."

"What?" Curly asked, eyes wide.

"I mean, *The* Castro, like in San Francisco," Caleb said.

"Well, say your partner is naked, and he's on his...."

"He means the fag neighborhood," Sylvester said, watching Caleb and ignoring the other two. Caleb nodded, smiling. "Why? What's there that will help us out of the spot you got us into?" He emphasized the "you."

"It's Halloween, tomorrow night," Caleb said. "Get it? Where would a freaky drag queen go on Halloween but to the Castro? That's where Drag Thing will be, for certain."

"We are not after Drag Thing. We are looking for Janet Jackle," Sylvester pointed out.

"And she is looking for Drag Thing," Caleb said. "She wants him as bad as we want her. I'm telling you: Janet

119

Jackle, Drag Thing, the Monster Cat—I will bet a dollar to a doughnut that's where we will find everyone tomorrow night."

"I don't see any doughnuts," Curly said, looking around hopefully. "I am kind of hungry, too." All the dirty talk had given him an appetite. It always did.

Sylvester managed one of his puckered mouth smiles (*Jeez, what did that mouth remind him of, Caleb wondered yet again?*). "You know, he said, "Maybe you are not as dumb as he looks. I think we will go trick or treating tomorrow."

"All right," Curly said, beaming. "That will be great. I missed out last year on account of I was in training, and the year before everybody was handing out apples. Like, who goes trick or treating for apples, anyway? Maybe I'll score some M&Ms this time."

* * * * * * *

For breakfast The Moes finished off the M&Ms and the ice cream, which was nothing now but soup, and the last couple of sardines, and washed it all down with what remained of the stale beer.

The pug looked a little dubiously at what they poured for her. Her stomach had churned the entire night; but finally she had a sip or two of beer and after that she seemed fine with this unorthodox feeding.

They left the pug at the Bat Cave, the door firmly shut to keep out the pack of dogs that had collected outside it, and drove to the Castro. As Hector had promised, the signs were already posted on telephone poles and trees near where they had "found" Fido: "Wanted—Honey Pot," the signs read, "Stolen from home. Generous reward for return. No questions asked." Beneath that was a picture of Honey Pot and a name—Todd—and a phone number.

"Bitchin'," Hector said. "That's our Fido, for sure."

"I don't know." Tom read the poster slowly, carefully forming the words with his lips. "It looks like him, totally, but it says here this dog's name is Honey Pot."

Hector smacked him on the back of his head. "It's a fucking alias, dickhead," he said. "Can't you read? This is like a wanted poster, ain't it? You wouldn't put your real name on a wanted poster, would you?"

"You're right. I never thought of that," Tom said, brightening. "Hyuk, hyuk, hyuk."

"You never thought, period. Come on." Hector tore the poster down from the pole and stuffed it in his pocket. "We'll call from the Bat Cave, case the FBI is listening. Good thing I got that cell phone."

* * * * * * *

Todd answered the call on the first ring—*like he was sitting on the phone*, Hector thought, which was encouraging. This guy really wanted his poochie back.

"We got your missing pooch," Hector said right off the bat. No point beating around the bush, as he saw it. "We didn't steal him, either, case you got any ideas, we found him fair and square."

"You fiend," the voice on the phone shouted. "You're a filthy, rotten pugnapper. I want my little Honey Pot back."

"I'm not a filthy whatever-you-called-it. I told you, we found the sorry mutt on the street, looked totally bummed out. We been taking care of him for you, too. Good care. Feeding him and everything."

"Liar!"

"Yeah, yeah, pants on fire, whatever. Anyway, relax, listen, you're gonna get him back, don't have a cow. Let's just talk a little business first, okay? Your sign says you're willing to pay a reward."

"Fifty dollars," Todd said.

"One hundred. And no questions asked."

"Listen," Todd's voice became concerned, "In case you didn't notice, Honey Pot is in heat. You have got to be really careful with her. You know what I'm saying?"

"Meat?" The connection was lousy. *Whoever paid for this phone got stiffed*, you asked him. It was criminal, the way things didn't work right today. People ought to be in the can for making all the crap that was out there. There was no justice in the world, if you asked him.

"Heat. Heat," Todd insisted, raising his voice. "You know, like hot?"

Hector glanced at the pooch. He was panting again, tongue hanging out one side of his mouth. "Yeah, I can see that," he said. "He looks hot."

"Well, I'm telling you, you have got to be careful. That dog is little, and very fragile. If the wrong guys got ahold of Honey Pot and they weren't careful, well, you know, it could be dangerous. Honey Pot could die from it."

The wrong guys? Jeez, who did this asshole think he was talking to, some kind of amateur? He had half a mind to tell the dude to fuck himself and hang up.

Except there was the money to think of, that was the important thing. This was business, after all. *Sticks and bones may take my something, something, something....* He could never remember the words to songs.

"Ah, don't worry about that," he said into the phone. "We're taking good care of the mutt, I'm telling you. You'll get him back in one piece."

"I had better. Just remember Honey Pot is in heat, and very little and very delicate. I am not paying a penny for a dead dog."

"Okay, okay, I read you. One hundred bucks, right?"

Todd sighed. "All right. One hundred. Where do I bring it?"

Like, he was going to give the guy the directions to the Bat Cave. That Connery dude would be there before Hector could put his whacker away. Ha, ha, what kind of a fool did this guy think he was talking to, anyway, like he'd fall for that?

"We'll come to you," he said instead. "Right now. Your place, okay?"

"No, I'm just leaving for work."

"So, then, where?"

"I'll tell you what: meet me outside Castro Mary's, the bar, at Eighteenth and Castro. Do you know where that is?"

"We can find it. Eighteenth and Castro, right?"

"Right. At ten o'clock, that's when I get off. And bring Honey Pot."

"Don't worry about that. Just be sure you bring the money, okay. And no funny business."

"I'll have your money," Todd said.

"Small bills, unmarked. And no cops," Hector said emphatically. "We see any cops, we're heading for Cuba. With your little Honey Pot."

Hector hung up. The other two looked at him questioningly. He nodded and they grinned all around.

"We're in business," he told them. "Dudes, you know what, we could make a killing on this shit. Say we snatched a dozen dogs a week, made a hundred bucks off of each one of them. That's…." He made an attempt at counting it off on his fingers. "A fucking lot of bucks," he finished, giving up on the arithmetic.

"How are we gonna get to Cuba?" Tom asked.

"That was just what they call poet's license," Hector said, "It don't mean anything. Who'd want to go there anyway, I heard they have this kinky thing they do with their beards. Besides, this guy will pay, don't worry about that, he wants the pooch back bad. Only," he added with a frown, "The dude said Fido here is hot, like he's overheated and we need to keep him cool or it would be trouble. Dude said he could die if we wasn't careful."

They all three looked at the pug. Honey Pot rolled her eyes at them and panted more earnestly. The ice cream and the M&Ms and the beer that had seemed so wonderful when she had gobbled them down a little while ago were sitting uncomfortably on her stomach.

"For sure he looks hot," Tom said.

"He looks sick," Archie said. "Bummer."

"Fuck. We don't want him to die on us," Hector said, really starting to worry now. "The dude's not gonna pay ransom on a dead dog. Here." He snatched up a *Playboy* magazine and shoved it at Archie. "Start fanning. We gotta cool him down."

Tom knelt down nose to nose with the pug and took a close look at her eyes. Honey Pot gave him a lopsided glance and continued to pant, tongue lolling to one side. Hector snatched up a Car and Driver and began to fan too.

"His eyes are all red," Tom said.

Honey Pot responded by suddenly hurling energetically in Tom's face. "Oh, man," he cried, wiping doggie barf from his face. "That is so totally gross."

"Fuck," Archie said from behind the pug. "I just noticed, his panties are all stained. Jesus, look at that. He's bleeding back here."

"Shit, he's dying," Hector wailed. "Fan harder."

* * * * * * *

"You're going as a pirate?" Teri asked, eyeing the costume that Peter was sewing up for himself.

"What's wrong with that?" he asked, pausing in mid-stitch.

"Oh, nothing. It's just, well, you see lots of pirates at Halloween. I was thinking something more, well, you know, the sort of thing where nobody would suspect it was you. Like, if you dressed up as a woman. A ballerina, maybe, or Mary Poppins."

"This is the Castro we are talking about, Teri," he said. "You think there won't be ballerinas galore? And we'll most likely be tripping over Mary Poppinses. Anyway, Lee specifically said he wanted me to dress macho. What could be more macho than a pirate?"

"Wonder Woman?" Teri offered, not very hopefully.

He grimaced disdainfully and went back to his sewing. "Oh, please, comic book characters, super mutants and mad scientists and all kinds of silliness. You know I don't go for that stuff. I just never believed in any of it, not even as a kid. This is real life, isn't it?"

Teri sighed and strapped on her gun. "Okay, you're the boss," she said resignedly. "I guess I will see you there, then." She and Jake had been assigned to the Castro for the evening, where the mobs of revelers sometimes got out of hand. "Give me a wave if you see me. What's Lee going as, by the way?"

124

"Lee? Oh, you know him, he will be the very picture of femininity, count on it. Nobody will out-spangle him. And speaking of the lovely Lee, I had better get busy, he will be here soon, and I promised to be ready and waiting."

* * * * * * *

"Sweets? Hello?" When there was no answer to his knock, Lee tried the door to Peter's apartment and, finding it unlocked, opened it gingerly and poked his head inside. It was not like Peter to forget a date. The man was far too anal for that.

"Knock, knock, anyone home?" he called. "Peter?" A single lamp glowed in the entryway; otherwise, the apartment was in darkness.

For a moment silence reigned. Then a voice that he almost-but-not-quite recognized called out from the living room, "Come on in, Ducks. I have been just dying to meet you."

"Meet me?" *What an odd thing to say.*

Lee stepped from the foyer into the darkened living room. A faint glow from the streetlights outside outlined the tightly closed window blinds. Something moved in front of them, a shadow among shadows.

A big shadow, the thought suddenly occurred to him. A little frisson of fear rippled up and down Lee's spine. Maybe someone had broken in and done something to Peter.

"Why are the lights off? What's going on?" he asked. His hand went instinctively to the wall switch and flicked it on. He blinked at the abrupt brightness, and, as his eyes adjusted, gasped. Standing before the window was the most enormous drag queen he had ever seen, eight feet tall at least, on towering sequined heels, with a wig that looked like Christmas tinsel and a face painted like something out of a child's coloring book.

"Hello, darling," the strange creature greeted him.

"It's-it's you," Lee stammered, staring goggle-eyed. "You're...."

"Drag Thing," she said, beaming. "I am ever so pleased to meet you, Ducks."

125

CHAPTER TEN

"Ready?" Caleb called from the hallway. "Ta da!" He jumped into the open doorway.

Curly farted resoundingly, *Kaboom!* Lawrence stared in stunned disbelieve. Even Sylvester was momentarily nonplussed at the bizarre sight before them: a six-foot tall winged mass of white feathers with enormous yellow feet. Only Caleb Wald's face, peering out from the avian apparition, was recognizable. Caleb spread his wings and flapped them noisily, and grinned.

"What do you think?" he asked.

A lady friend who happened to be a dressmaker had made the costume for him, sewing much of the night. It had not been entirely free, however, since he had had to service her before she would finish it. She was a little, round thing who had huffed and puffed her way through the sex—a full hour of humping and thumping and *Huff* and *Puff* and *Grunt* until she had finally signaled her finish in a series of *Moan, Urk, and Gurgle* in his ear and *Ooohs* that had threatened his hearing. Afterward, she had patted him like a puppy and said, "You did a good job, honey."

And people thought it was easy being a major stud! If they only knew what he went through, he thought grimly.

Still, the results were worth the effort. He was every inch a bird, from the yellow bird shoes, like two-foot-long chicken feet, to the crest atop his head, and enough white feathers in between to retrofit an entire flock of geese. The enormous wings strapped to his arms spread six feet when opened, and when he flapped them now for effect, they made a loud *whooshing* noise and created a considerable breeze.

Once he had gotten over the shock, Curly at least was impressed. "Wowee," he said in evident admiration. "That is really far out."

"I have never seen anything like it," Lawrence said. "Honest, I mean that sincerely. Nothing even close."

"Only, I would have made the beak yellow, too," Curly said.

"I am not wearing a beak," Caleb replied in a frosty voice.

"Really?" Curly peered more intently.

"So tell me," Sylvester said, "Why are you dressed like a duck?"

"It is not a duck. It is an owl," Caleb said in a petulant voice. "You know, the symbol of wisdom." Sylvester grunted and pursed his lips.

"What about you guys, aren't you going to dress up?" Caleb asked, looking their dark suits up and down. "We're going to the Castro. It's Halloween, for Christ's sake. Everyone will be in costume."

"We are representatives of the United States Government," Sylvester said. "We have to maintain a certain dignity at all times. We would not want to embarrass the president, after all."

Caleb, who was not especially impressed with their brand of dignity, said, "Yeah, sure, whatever."

Personally he thought maybe they were adequately costumed as it was—they looked like a trio of clowns, in his opinion. He smoothed his feathers with one hand.

* * * * * * *

Lee was wearing a rhinestone tiara with ostrich feathers that quivered three feet in the air, and a full-length gown of sequined crimson, with white satin pumps and long white gloves. It was, he had explained, his Merry Widow costume.

"My friend Luis was supposed to drive us there in his ambulance, but he's not answering his cell phone. Knowing him, he's probably holed up with someone in a cop uniform," Lee said as they exited Peter's apartment. "Oh,

sweetie, I just know this is going to be the night of a life-
time." He began to hum a snippet of Vilja.

"It is going to be a memorable night for someone of our
acquaintance," Drag Thing said. "I have to make a little stop
before we go out."

"Here?" Lee said in surprise. Drag Thing had stopped at
a door down the hall. "That's the Kravitz's apartment, isn't
it?"

"Exactly. I have a little business to finish with Mr.
Kravitz. Why don't you go on downstairs and wait for me by
the front door."

"Can't I stay and watch?" Lee had a score or two of his
own he would like to settle with the Kravitz couple. "Pretty
please?"

"Well, if you must, but only from the doorway," Drag
Thing conceded. "We don't want your plumes soiled." She
rapped on the Kravitz door.

It was Gladys who answered. Her glance went first to
Lee, who was, after all, more or less at her own height. She
glowered disapprovingly at his costume. A red dress, and a
tiara with feathers—and he still had that beard. Sometimes
she wanted to just pull it out, hair by hair.

Gradually, however, she became aware that he was not
alone. She tilted her head back, slowly raising her eyes, until
she was looking Drag Thing square in the face.

"Hello, toots," Drag Thing said, neon lips spreading ear
to ear. "We've come to call on your hubby. Is he free?"

Gladys, her nerves already overwrought, gave one small
shriek. Her eyes rolled back into her head, and she keeled
over backwards like a fallen tree.

"Gladys? Did you yell?" Abner Kravitz opened the bathroom door and appeared in it naked, toweling himself dry. "I
thought I heard someone call."

"A little birdie told me you had been bad, Mister
Kravitz," Drag Thing said, stepping over Gladys' prone body
and into the apartment. "I have come to spanky, spanky the
naughty boy."

Abner's mouth fell open and his eyes went wide. "Holy
shit," he cried. He dashed for the bedroom, but Drag Thing

128

had crossed the living room in three giant strides and was there before him, blocking the way.

"Now, now," she said, "We mustn't be coy. This won't take long. Sooner begun, sooner ended, as they say."

Abner made a run for the front door, but Lee, in full regalia, was standing in that opening. In Abner's terrified imagination, Lee looked nearly as gigantic and as frightening as Drag Thing did. He stopped abruptly, seeing, for the first time, his wife unconscious on the floor.

"Gladys," he cried, "What have they done to you? You bastards."

His eyes darted about the room wildly. There was only one other exit available to him, the open window. He rushed to that and scrambled over the sill, to the fire escape outside.

"Hmm," Drag Thing said, with a shrug. "Someone does not want to play, it seems." She went to the window.

"Stay away from me," a naked Abner said, cowering against the fire escape railing and trying to conceal his genitals behind a trembling hand.

"You perverts," a woman's voice shouted from across the way. A window slammed shut and blinds were hastily closed.

"Do what you want with my wife. Believe me, she won't feel a thing, she never does." Abner cried when Drag Thing moved as if to climb out the window. "Just leave me alone."

"Oh, well, if you wish," Drag Thing said. She pulled the window down instead and latched it. "But it might get a little warm out there."

She paused at the telephone long enough to dial the police, and when they answered, she said, "There is a terrorist on my fire escape, and he says he has a bomb concealed on his person and is going to blow up the building. Please send help as quickly as possible."

She replaced the receiver before any questions could be asked, and coming to the front door, linked her arm in Lee's.

"I'd say we have about five minutes till show time," Drag Thing said. "Why don't we see if we can find a front row seat in that building across the way?"

In the distance, they could already hear the wail of sirens.

* * * * * * *

Gladys regained consciousness slowly. At first, dazed, she had no memory of what had transpired or why she was on the floor. She sat up, shaking her head, and looked around. Standing just a few feet from her was an enormous bird, a goose, she thought, but the size of a man. She clamped a hand over her mouth and looked for Abner.

"You perverts," a voice cried from across the street. "I see what you're doing over there."

Gladys saw her husband then, bent naked over the back of the living room sofa, his bottom in the air, while three dark suited men...she blinked her eyes, disbelieving. What on earth were they doing? Surely they weren't...

"Abner," she cried with a shriek, and fainted again.

* * * * * * *

"I still don't see," Caleb said, "Why you thought he would have had a bomb hidden there."

"Homeland Security is trained to be thorough," Sylvester said. "The caller said he had a bomb concealed on his person and that was the only possible place of concealment. We had to be sure."

"Well, what kind of explosives could he have had hidden up his backside?" Caleb asked.

"You would be surprised," Sylvester said.

Lawrence nudged Curly with an elbow and winked. Curly let fly one of his more horrific outbursts. *Kapow!*

"Case in point," Sylvester said dryly.

"Jesus," was Caleb's remark. He fanned the air vigorously with one wing while pinching his nose tightly with his free hand.

Sylvester drove, but he had to park the car while they were still several blocks from the Castro. The traffic at this point was bumper to bumper and barely moving. "I'm afraid this is close as we are going to get," he said. "We will have to walk from here." He parked in an illegal spot and hung a handicapped card over the mirror. Part of their kit. Homeland provided for every contingency.

Walking, however, was not the easiest task either, not in two-foot long plastic bird's feet, as Caleb quickly discovered. *No wonder pigeons walk funny*, he thought. He found himself settling into a kind of waddle that sent his tail feathers swaying wildly to and fro. The good thing was, the people behind him quickly learned to keep their distance to avoid getting swatted by feathers. That at least was a plus—the closer they got to the Castro, the thicker the crowds became, until they were fairly shoving their way through an elbow-to-elbow throng.

"I'm hungry," Curly announced out of the blue. That bomb search a little earlier had worked up an appetite.

"Me too," Lawrence agreed.

"Yeah, we had better eat before we get there," Caleb said, "You think this crowd is something, wait until we reach Castro Street. Things will be really crazy there."

Sylvester, who had long since trained himself to subsist on the leanest of rations, would like to have insisted that they press on, but he knew from experience that once the other two focused on their appetites there was little hope of their thinking of anything else until they were satisfied, and he needed them alert for whatever might await them when they reached their destination. He hated to give Wald any credit, but he suspected he might just be right in suggesting the Castro for their investigation. He hoped he was. They needed results, and they needed them now. Already, the Agency was getting impatient.

"There's a take out just up there. We'll get something to go and eat it on the way," he said, pointing to a big sign with a picture of a handsome young delivery boy and the message, "Don't go out tonight, call Chicken Delight."

They waited what seemed an interminable time in the fast food line. Caleb was uncomfortably aware that he was the center of much attention. Christ, he wondered, hadn't these idiots ever seen anyone in costume before? Well, yes, there were plenty of costumes on display: two gypsy ladies, a pirate, two guys in tacky drag—even a big pink watermelon dotted with black seeds. But no birds.

That must be it, he thought, *it's the feathers. Fuck 'em,* he decided, steadfastly ignoring the increasingly pointed stares and the titters.

Finally it was their turn at the counter. An acne-afflicted young man in a red and white shirt and a straw hat with a cockscomb atop it greeted them without enthusiasm. "What'll it be, ladies?" he asked, "And don't take all night, there's others behind you."

Lawrence and Curly ordered Cluckaburgers with the works and Chicken Fried Fries, and Sylvester ordered just a cup of coffee. They stepped aside for Caleb. He swished up to the counter, tail feathers sweeping the floor.

"I'll have the My Big Fat Hen Sandwich with the works," he said, studying the menu posted behind the counter.

"Isn't that like, some kind of cannibalism, Mister Chicken?" the order clerk asked, looking Caleb's feathery finery up and down with a smirk.

"I'm not a chicken, you idiot, I'm an owl," Caleb replied. He snatched the bag out of the grinning clerk's hand and strode imperiously for the door—or, as imperiously as he could manage in plastic feet and swaying tail feathers.

"Cock-a-doodle-Do," the counter man called after him, flapping his elbows. There was a roar of laughter from the other patrons, which Caleb stoically ignored.

"Ignoramuses," he muttered under his breath.

They ate as they walked, Curly and Lawrence making loud slurping noises and Sylvester sipping his coffee decorously. They had gone about a block further when Caleb suddenly cried, "Whoa, wait a second," and stopped abruptly. The trio of agents stopped with him.

"What?" Lawrence demanded sharply, automatically reaching for his gun. He was trained to shoot first and investigate later.

"There. The dog," Caleb said, pointing at a huge Great Dane tied by his leash to a telephone pole just outside of a noisy bar.

"What about him?" Sylvester asked, puzzled.

"That Jackle dame has She Cat with her—the pussy from hell," Caleb said. "We need a dog, a big dog. If we find her, we can sic the dog on the cat while we handle the Jackle broad."

Sylvester studied the Great Dane. It was true: the dog was large, enormous, in fact. That was the only thing about him however that suggested ferocity. His tail wagged in happy greeting and he appeared to be grinning at them open-mouthed, his tongue hanging out and dribbling saliva. Even more telling, he was wearing a huge lavender ribbon around his neck, and his toenails were painted to match.

"I am not altogether sure that a dog with lavender toe-nails is the type to sic on cats," Sylvester said.

"Forget about the toenails," Caleb said. "I'm telling you, all dogs hate cats, it's in their blood. When this dog sees She Cat he's going to go for her throat." He untied the dog's leash. "Come on Rover."

The dog cast a considering glance in the direction of the bar. Loud music drifted through the door as a tipsy patron stepped outside to light a cigarette. He gave the group on the sidewalk no more than a passing glance. His "gaydar" told him they were straight. Anyway, the three suited ones were unattractive, and the fourth one couldn't be seen for feathers. The dog was the only one with style. You could never go wrong with a lavender bow, after all. The stranger lit his cigarette with a platinum lighter and turned his attention in-stead to the passing parade, checking out a cute guy in a sailor costume.

"Nice buns," he said aloud. The sailor looked back to grin at him, but he kept going.

"Jeez, making remarks like that in public," Caleb said. "These guys are sick, you ask me."

Curly shrugged and gave Lawrence a glance. Lawrence winked at him again. He had agreed with the assessment of the sailor's buns. They were nice—"But yours are nicer," he leaned close to whisper in Curly's ear. *Ffftt. Kaboom, Pow*, was the response.

"Let's go, mutt," Caleb said, tugging on the dog's leash. "Jesus." He gave Curly a dirty look.

"What if his owner comes out?" Sylvester asked. For a troublesome moment, he had thought that the guy lighting his cigarette might be the owner. Their standing orders were to avoid public disturbances—that was why he had intervened when Caleb had stupidly assaulted that woman outside the bar. They could not afford to have Caleb arrested, and certainly not tonight, while he was dressed as a chicken. It would be very difficult to explain stealing a dog to his superiors, let alone the feathers, and he was hoping for a promotion in the near future—so he would not again have to work a case with imbeciles like the two with him on this one.

"Once we get a half a block away from here, the owner would never be able to spot us in this mob," Caleb said. "Come on, trust me, this dog is what we need." He tugged again at the leash and when the animal still did not budge, Caleb tore off a chunk of his Big Fat Hen Sandwich. The dog wolfed it down in one gulp and looked expectantly at the rest.

"Fly now, pay later," Caleb said. This time when he pulled on the leash, the dog gave a shake of his head and fell into step beside Caleb, his eyes still on the sandwich, his vigil outside the bar forgotten. In his Great Dane-ish mind, every five minutes was a new day. This day was focused on Big Fat Hen Sandwiches. The bar was the previous day.

The crowd got still thicker as they approached Castro Street, ground zero for Halloween festivities, until they were moving along with a solid mass of others. Caleb worried about his tail feathers, and tried not to step on any toes with his bird feet, not out of courtesy, but from fear that he would trip. If you fell on the sidewalk in this mob of fruits, you could get trampled before you could get back up. It was like the running of the bulls at that place in Italy, Pamplemousse they called it. You took your life in your hands. Especially an owl.

Makeshift gates had been set up in the middle of the street two blocks before they got to Castro Street, with signs suggesting a three-dollar donation. A big burly dyke in leather, dripping with chains and her arms covered with tattoos, eyed them warily as they approached the gate, Caleb and the Great Dane in the lead.

134

"Three dollars," she greeted them.

"It's a donation, right? I don't actually *have* to pay, do I?" Caleb asked. "I mean, a donation means voluntary, doesn't it?"

The dyke looked him up and down. "Three bucks," she said. "Each. The dog gets in for free."

"Listen, I need to ask you," Caleb said, "I am looking for someone. Have you seen a drag queen go through here tonight? A really big one. Really ugly."

"You just flew in from Kansas, right?" the disbelieving dyke asked. "This is the Castro, sweetheart, it is Halloween. If you laid every big ugly drag queen in there end to end they would probably be tickled pink."

"Nah, you don't get it," Caleb said. "I am talking about someone really, *really* weird looking."

"Let me get this straight," she said, "You are dressed as a duck, you have got a Great Dane with a lavender ribbon and lavender toenails on a leash, and three Homeland Security agents in black suits glued to your butt, and you are asking me if I have seen someone weird?"

"How did you know we were Homeland Security agents?" Sylvester asked.

"Oh, puh-leeze." She raised an eyebrow.

"And I am not a duck," Caleb said, "I'm an owl."

"Well, excuse me, that certainly puts my mind at ease," she said, "For a minute there I thought you had transcended the borders of good taste. And nobody wears that much black unless he's an undertaker or Homeland Security, and they don't look bright enough to be undertakers. Besides, undertakers don't usually partner with ducks."

"Okay, let me ask you this, then—have you seen a lesbian?" Caleb asked. "Really big. Really ugly. With an enormous pussy?"

The dyke sighed and rolled her eyes. "Three dollars. Each," she said. "The dog gets in free."

CHAPTER ELEVEN

"Man, you ever see so many people?" Tom asked, looking everywhere. They were on Castro Street, in the middle of the street because the sidewalks were all but impassable.

"Fuckin' fags, must be a million of 'em," Hector said.

"You think that's the place?" Archie asked, indicating a bar just off to their right where the patrons overflowed through the open doors onto the sidewalks.

"Nah, the sign over the door says that's The Five and Dime. We're looking for Castro Mary's," Hector said.

"There's a couple of hot babes over there, checking us out," Archie said, nodding in their direction.

"They're not babes, they're drag queens," Hector said. "You peckerhead."

Archie looked again. One of the "girls" waved at him and blew a kiss. "Hey, there, handsome," she called in a baritone voice. "I'm Veronica and this is my girlfriend, Betty. Where you going?"

He grinned and started to wave back, until he saw Hector shoot him a furious glance. Archie dropped his hand and replaced the grin with a scowl. "Well, they sure look like hot babes," he said.

"Don't be turning homo on me," Hector said.

"Fuck you." Archie thought for a moment. "Anyway, I'll bet they were smiling at the pooch." Hector was carrying Honey Pot in his arms. "Yeah, you got that right, he is sure one cute little doggie, isn't he?" Tom said. He frowned. "You know, maybe you shouldn't be carrying him out in plain sight like that, though. What if the cops are watching for us? Say like that Todd dude has called in the Connery guy and his buddies?"

136

"Now, you know, that's the first bright idea you've had," Hector said. "Here, put him inside your jacket." He handed Honey Pot to Tom.

"What if he starts bleeding again?" Tom said doubtfully.

"What, you're afraid of a little blood, you wuss? Put his panties back on him, then. You saving them for a souvenir or what?"

Tom, who had sort of thought maybe he would keep them—not everyone would know they had come off a doggie—reluctantly took them from his pocket and struggled to slip them onto Honey Pot's hind legs. She wriggled and tried to lick his face.

"Get out," he said, but he laughed anyway. He was sure a cute little pooch. In a way he was sorry they had to give him back. Of course, there was the money to think of: A hundred bucks. He'd never seen that much money at one time. Who would have thought it? Hector was as mean as cat piss but he was truly a wise dude. There was no denying it.

He gave up on trying to get the panties on the pooch. Anyway, he really had kind of hoped to keep them for a souvenir. He glanced in Hector's direction, but Hector was busy looking for the bar, Castro Mary's, where they were supposed to meet Fido's owner. Tom tucked the panties down inside the back of his gangbanger pants instead.

Something bumped against his leg and he looked down to see that they had been joined by a Springer Spaniel. The Spaniel looked longingly up at Honey Pot and darted in and out between Tom's feet.

"Hey, careful, there," Tom said, almost tripping over him.

"Little guy wants to play," Archie said. "Ain't that cute. Fido is sure a popular little mutt. I still say he's like one of the Moes."

"Yeah. Maybe we should keep him," Tom said tentatively. That was what he had secretly been wishing for, but he had been kind of afraid to suggest it until Archie brought it up.

"What the fuck, you crazy? You know how much money a hundred bucks is?" Hector said.

Tom, who actually didn't know, said, "Yeah. You're right." Another dog, a mixed breed, joined the Springer. "Sure is a popular little dude, though."

* * * * * * *

"Man, this is sure a popular place," Jake said. "Are we looking for anything in particular?"

"No, just keep your eyes open for any sign of trouble," Teri said. "Oh, well, yes, if you see that Drag Thing, I think we ought to take him in on that mugging, even though I am not entirely convinced those guys were telling the truth the other night."

"We didn't get statements from them," Jake said. "Without any witnesses, it would end up just Drag Thing's word against that Wald guy's, and frankly, Wald struck me as pretty flaky."

"I agree," Teri said. "Still…we'll see what Drag Thing has to say—if we spot him. It is hard to imagine he would not show up here, though. Halloween. The Castro. Gosh, look at these mobs."

"He could be standing right next to us, and we might not see him," Jake said.

"Man, those are great cop costumes," a sailor said, giving Jake in particular the eye. "How about a mutual strip search, officer?"

Jake started to laugh, but caught Teri's eye and assumed a stern expression instead. "Watch it, fella," he said in his deepest baritone. Too bad, though. The sailor had been kind of hot. Nice buns, too.

* * * * * * *

"That's the best turkey costume I've ever seen," a passing Spider Man said to Caleb.

"It's not a turkey," Caleb snapped. "It's an owl, damn it," but Spider Man had already vanished into the mob.

The Great Dane suddenly gave a mighty tug on his leash.

138

"Whoa, there," Caleb yelled, taking a couple of little jigging steps as he tried to hold the dog in check. "Rover's on the scent of something. This might be it. I'll bet it's that She-Cat."

"Maybe you should let him go," Sylvester said.

"Maybe I don't have any choice," Caleb said, feeling as if his arms were being pulled out of their sockets as the Dane lunged insistently forward. The leash slipped from Caleb's hands, and in a moment, the dog was gone into the crowd with one might woof and a clickety clack of lavender toe-nails on the pavement.

"After him," Caleb cried, but before he could go more than a step or two, someone had blocked his way—or rather, some*thing*, something enormous and wearing a blue dress covered in sequins.

* * * * * * *

"Honey Pot!" a voice shouted, and a short-legged man in an orange tank top ran up to the Moes. "Give her to me."

He snatched the pug out of Tom's hands and hugged her with delight. "My poor baby, daddy has been so worried, did the mean men hurt you, my little sweetie pie pooh." He gave her a big kiss. Honey Pot licked his face in return and wagged her tail enthusiastically.

"The mutt is fine," Hector said, stepping to the fore. "Now fork over the bread. One hundred dollars, and no tricks."

Todd reached for his wallet, but before he could get it, a huge Great Dane with a lavender bow at his neck and toe-nails to match bounded out of the crowd and gave a mighty leap at Tom.

Caught unexpected, Tom fell to his knees on the side-walk. The Dane sniffed enthusiastically at his backside and immediately jumped atop him and began to hump him frantically.

"Hey, get him off," Tom shouted, trying unsuccessfully to crawl away, His low rider pants, already perched at a precarious level on his scrawny hips, slipped downward to bare his snow white bottom "Fucking beast is trying to dick me, get him off. Ouch, hey, not my butt hole, you fucking queer! Get him off!"

"Okay, you guys, hold it right there," someone shouted. Two cops, a man and a woman, ran up. "Sorry fellas, what you do in private is your business, but no sex action in public," Jake said sternly. "Bestiality or otherwise."

"Jesus, like he's my date, or what?" Tom cried, wriggling frantically, which only inspired the Great Dane to increase his efforts. "Hey, hey, quit, I tell you, stop."

Two more dogs had jumped into the fray, a Springer trying to get in place alongside the Dane and a big mongrel who decided he would start at the opposite end. He placed his paws atop Tom's head and began to thrust energetically at his face.

"Hey, get that away from me," Tom said, "I ain't into sucking cock, and not especially no doggie cock, you four legged pervert."

"Whose dogs are these?" Teri demanded. "Who's running this live sex show?"

"Hector's the boss, tell 'em, Hector," Tom wailed. "Ow, oof, get this monster off my butt. Hey, not in my face, you fucking mutt." He dropped his face into his hands. Undeterred, the mongrel continued to hump his scalp.

"Hey, can I help it if the dogs got a boner for this dickhead?" Hector said. "I guess he's just the type turns doggies on. As for me, I was just talking some business with our buddy here." He jerked a thumb in Todd's direction.

"Arrest him, officer," Todd cried indignantly, clutching Honey Pot to his chest and pointing an accusing finger. "That monster was trying to get money for my Honey Pot."

"He's peddling your honey pot? So, prostitution, too," Jake said. "And live sex shows, dog stuff, right out here on the street. Buddy, you are in some real trouble." He took hold of Hector's arm. "And, you, down there on the sidewalk," he said to Tom, "break it off. I'm ordering you. The orgy is over."

"Make 'em quit, Hector" Tom wailed. "Ouch, oh, no, don't."

Archie backed slowly away from all this activity. He was thinking that if he could get just a little further, he could be gone in the crowd. Half a block, and they would never find him. Things looked like they were getting seriously out of hand here. If he got busted again he was in deep shit. He hadn't shown for his last couple of appointments with his parole officer.

"Hey, honey," someone said in a stage whisper at his side, and he looked around to discover the two drag queens who had been giving him the eye earlier.

"I'm Veronica," the dark haired one said, winking at him and taking hold of Archie's arm, "And this is Betty. And our apartment is right over there, if you were thinking about making a getaway."

"Veronica and I just love company," Betty said. "Especially man company."

"Especially cute man company," Veronica said.

Hector was struggling with the two cops now. As Archie watched, undecided, Hector managed to get his hands free, and he made one of those mistakes people sometimes make when under pressure. By the merest chance, he found his flailing hand on the guy cop's gun. On an impulse, Hector yanked the gun from its holster and fired it into the air. People in the crowd began to scream and shove at one another, trying to get away.

Oh, man, the poop is going to really hit the fan now, Archie thought. He smiled down at the drag queen holding his arm. "Think I'm man enough?" he asked Veronica.

"You'll do," she said, smiling back. Betty grabbed Archie's other arm and between them the two lovelies whisked Archie quickly away.

Hector was struggling in earnest with the two cops now and Tom was still being energetically humped, front and back, by a growing horde of dogs. No one noticed Archie disappearing through the door with the two drag queens. In a moment, they were inside.

"Whew," he said, "Thanks for saving my butt."

"Your butt is our pleasure. Are you a jughead?" Veronica asked.

"No, my names Archie," he said.

"She meant, a marine," Betty said. "And it's jarhead, honey, I wish you'd get it right."

Veronica shrugged. "Jughead, jarhead, I don't care what you call them, the point is, they're bottoms. All these nelly Castro queens want to be on top. It so gets to be a bore."

"Oh, hey," Archie said. Betty had groped him.

"Never mind, girl," she said, "I'm sure this is going to work out very nicely. That's pretty impressive, Jughead."

"Archie," he said. He hesitated for no more than a moment. Outside was nothing but trouble. Anyway, it had been a while since he'd gotten laid and Betty's hand was producing quick results—and, truth to tell, he never had been all that picky about the minor details. The two drag queens were total babes. So what if they weren't real women? He was a real man, wasn't he? That was the important thing, and their sex didn't change that.

"You ain't seen nothin' yet," he said, grinning.

They grabbed both his arms again and hustled him up the stairs.

"I'll bet we're going to, though," Betty said with a giggle.

* * * * * * *

Jake had just finally gotten the cuff on a struggling, cursing Hector when more shots rang out nearby, followed by another chorus of screams. Teri grabbed for her gun. This was crazy. She had never seen the Castro so hopping.

"You go ahead and check that out," Jake said, "Don't worry, I can take care of this joker"

"Hey," Tom sobbed, pinned to the sidewalk. A mob of dogs—twenty or thirty of them by this time—crowded around him, dancing and woofing for their turn. "That fucking hound just got my cherry."

Dark brown Birkenstocks appeared in his line of vision, and Tom looked up, but a pair of bobbing canine balls temporarily blocked his view. A French poodle had replaced the mongrel atop his head. Tom pushed the doggy testicles rudely aside, eliciting an enthusiastic *arf, arf, arf, arf* from their owner, and a torrent of something wet and sticky on his scalp.

142

Tom looked up. What he saw was a bearded man with a priest's collar looking down at him.

"Repent," the stranger said in a sepulchral voice. "You have surely strayed, my son, but I tell you truly, redemption awaits you. You have only to admit that what you are doing is wrong."

"You're telling me," Tom said plaintively "This is about as wrong as it gets, you want my opinion. I done trains before but I was never the station."

"Do you sincerely wish to change your ways?" the stranger demanded.

"Absolutely," Tom said fervently. An ambitious Scottie tried to take the Great Dane's place behind him, hopping wildly up and down on his too-short legs.

"And you truly are ready for this, this abomination you are doing, to end?" the stranger said, looking both surprised and delighted.

"Ready? Shit, it can't end soon enough for me," Tom said, trying to shoo away with one hand a Chihuahua who had replaced the French Poodle and could reach no higher than an eyebrow, which apparently deterred him not at all. He went to town energetically.

"Then I can happily tell you that there is another path that you can follow in lieu of this one," the stranger said.

"Show me the way, please, padre" Tom said. "I'm ready to boog. I swear it. This shit sucks."

A hand reached down for him. Tom seized it and scrambled to his feet, the dogs falling away. The Great Dane, having done what he had come to do, jumped up to place his front paws on Tom's chest, almost knocking him down again, and gave him a sloppy but grateful tongue-kiss.

"Fuck off," Tom said, kneeing him. "You ought to have kissed me before hand, you horny bastard." He tugged his pants up.

"I'm Father Flinnigan, of The Heartfelt Hands," the priest said, shaking Tom's hand up and down heartily, his beard bobbing with each hand pump. "Our business is lost souls, and we have an animal shelter as well. I see you are good with dogs. If you would care to join with us, I can promise we will give you a good home and spiritual guidance to go with it."

"A home?" Tom said, shoving a late coming Beagle aside. He thought of the Bat Cave with its urine smells and mildew. "You mean, like a real bed, and regular meals, and stuff like that?"

"I will welcome you as if you were my own son," Father Flinnigan said. Although he had managed to amass dogs galore in his two years with the mission, he had yet to bring in a single human convert. To find this wayward young man tonight, eager to repent his sinful ways and join him, was like a miracle. He couldn't have been more thrilled. "I will be a father to you," he vowed in a voice trembling with emotion.

Tom ran his hand through his hair and brought it back with a grimace. "Yech," he said, staring at his hand, "Look what that fucking mutt did in my hair."

He glanced past Father Flinnigan. Archie had disappeared somewhere, and so had the woman cop, and the man cop was reading a still swearing, handcuffed Hector his rights. For the moment, the coast was clear.

"Daddy, I'm all yours," Tom said to his new benefactor. "Can we, like, head for home now?"

* * * * * * *

"You," Caleb said with a gasp, looking up into Drag Thing's audaciously painted face.

"Why, it is the naughty man, isn't it?" Drag Thing said. "The naughty man that told terrible fibs about Drag Thing."

"Arrest him," Caleb cried, looking at the three agents, but before anyone could move, another enormous creature with a mop of coppery hair and what looked like a badly groomed mountain lion on a chain suddenly leaped from between two buildings to confront them. The cat snarled ominously and strained at the chain holding her.

"Aha," Janet Jackle yelled, her eyes flashing maniacally, "So you're Drag Thing? I've found you at last. Well, bitch, I have a score to settle with you. You nearly killed my Melissa. Now you will have Missy Hyde to answer to."

144

"Jesus, look at that pussy, it's huge," Lawrence said, so bug-eyed he completely forgot about drawing his gun.

"Is that what they look like?" Curly asked, blinking "I never saw one before. It's not very pretty, is it? And it doesn't look anything like the picture in the coloring book."

"My pussy is not pretty, but she is very voracious," Janet Jackle said.

"What's that mean, what she called it?" Curly asked Lawrence in a loud whisper.

"It means it eats things," Lawrence said.

"I thought it was...."

"Let me show you, Mister Scrub," Janet interrupted them with a cackle of glee. She bent down and unclasped She Cat's chain. "Oh, beautiful pussy, oh pussy my love, what a beautiful pussy you are," she crooned. She pointed a finger at Drag Thing and cried, "Go, Missy Hyde. Attack! Kill! Kill Drag Thing!"

"Grrr, Meow, Grrrr," Missy Hyde roared in eager anticipation, saliva drooling from her fangs. She crouched, topaz eyes gleaming—and leaped, not at Drag Thing, but at Caleb, landing on his chest and knocking him flat to the ground.

Lee tugged at Drag Thing's sleeve. "I think it's time we went trick or treating," he whispered.

"I think you are wise," Drag Thing agreed.

"Awk, eek, urk," Caleb squawked like a wounded parrot, feathers flailing, "Get this monster off of me." He struggled to fend off the claws that threatened to rip his face open, and saw with terrified eyes the shining fangs coming closer his throat. The memory of the times he had taunted the cat flashed before his eyes.

"Your gun, you moron," Sylvester said, whacking Lawrence's arm. "Shoot the cat before it kills Wald."

Lawrence had been occupied with explaining things to a fascinated Curly. Now, looking around, he immediately grasped Caleb's plight. "Jesus," he swore. The cat was about to eat the bird. He palmed his gun, took quick aim, and fired.

She Cat gave a shriek of pain and leaped into the air. For a second or two, she turned her malevolent eyes on Lawrence. Terrified, he backed up hastily, tripped over Curly's feet and fell on his back. Before he could regain his balance or shoot again, She Cat had taken a mighty leap, over Caleb's prone figure and charged into the costumed Castro crowd. Screaming, the terrified Halloween revelers parted to make way for the beast, and in a moment she was gone.

"You've hurt my pussy," Janet cried. "You—you dick!"

Lawrence was halfway to his feet. She slapped the gun out of his hand and knocked him to the sidewalk again. Stunned, he landed beside Caleb.

"Hey, you can't do that to my partner," Curly shouted, putting his hands angrily on his hips. "Play fair." For once, no one even noticed his indignant fart.

Janet would have done far more than knock people down. She was mad enough, and felt strong enough, to rip them to shreds, all four of them, and she would have done so in a minute, but her thoughts were on the wounded She-Cat. Melissa's child. She must save her.

"Come back, come back, Missy Hyde, come back to The Five And Dime," she called, pushing and shoving her way through the terrified crowds after her. "Oh, she's gone," she sobbed in frustration.

She paused momentarily to look over her shoulder. "It's all your fault, you monster," she said to Drag Thing. "You, you horrible…where is she? Where is Drag Thing?"

Drag Thing, however, had vanished as well.

CHAPTER TWELVE

"Where are we going?" Lee asked, panting. Running in a tight skirt and stilettos was never easy, and trying to keep up with Drag Thing's long-legged flight made it doubly so.

"Away, away," Drag Thing cried merrily, enjoying herself immensely. She hadn't had this much fun since the night she had met Mister Moe and Mister Moe and Mister Moe. "We must, we must, they're after us, the Owl and the Pussy from hell, and Jackle and Hyde as well. We must away, I say, to save the day."

"Drag Thing. Stop. Hold it right there," a female voice commanded from behind them.

Drag Thing halted as ordered and looked around in the direction of the voice. "Why, it's the police person," she cried, grinning with delight. "It's Miss Teri. I was supposed to wave when I saw you." She did so, lifting one meaty hand into the air and waving it with sufficient force to create a small breeze that ruffled Teri's hair.

"How...?" Teri blinked and stammered her surprise. "How do you know me?" she asked. "How do you know my name?"

"Why, Miss Lovely and I," Drag Thing started to say, but when she looked around, she realized she was alone. Lorelie Lee had gone. "Oh, she seems to have disappeared. I must find her, before they do." She started to move away, but she turned back briefly once again. "Be a dear, won't you," she said, "and if you see this great big pussy coming down the street, do try to head it off. I'm afraid it's after me." She started again, and paused once more. "Or an owl," she added. "He's after me too. Or three undertakers.

They're—well, it seems as if everybody is after poor Drag Thing. It's the naughty man's fault."

"Wait," Teri ordered, but Drag Thing ignored her, peering to and fro in search of the companion who had been with her only a moment before and who, Terri had just a fleeting impression, had looked suspiciously like Lorelie Lee in one of his many drag incarnations.

Teri started to raise her gun, and hesitated. She couldn't fire into the crowd, certainly, but that wasn't what kept her from going after Drag Thing. Something about that face, the voice…she couldn't quite put her finger on it. While she vacillated, Drag Thing hurried down the street and was quickly lost to sight.

Watching from a sheltered doorway a short distance off, Janet Jackle pursed her lips thoughtfully. Why had the cop lady started to take Drag Thing into custody, and then changed her mind and let her go?

The policewoman returned her gun to her holster. She continued to stare thoughtfully after Drag Thing, but made no effort to pursue her.

This, Janet thought, will bear some watching. *Something is rotten in the neighborhood, Mister Rogers.*

* * * * * * *

"Psst. Here."

Drag Thing looked in the direction of the sibilant whisper and found Lorelie Lee sheltered in the doorway of a bookstore.

"Oh, there you are," Drag Thing said, relieved, "I was afraid I had lost you."

"Quick, we can hide in here," Lee said. He grabbed Drag Thing's arm and tugged her into the bookstore.

"What a brilliant idea," Drag Thing said, thoroughly delighted. "I've been in this shop before. We can simply pretend we are customers and no one will pay us the slightest heed."

Lee gave his eight-and-one-half-foot companion a measuring look. "Somehow I doubt that they won't notice us," he said.

148

"Trust me," Drag Thing insisted, leading them to a table piled high with stacks of books. The sign hanging above the table read "Sexual Studies." "This looks appropriate," she said. "I'll stand on this side, and you stand there, and try to look as if you know nothing."

"Well, that should be easy, at least," Lee said dryly, taking his place beside a tall stack of books and trying to look inconspicuous—not the easiest task in the world with a mile high platinum wig and a full beard, to say nothing of a tiara with ostrich feathers.

They had barely gotten into their positions before a spare, bookish looking man approached them. "Excuse me, ladies," he said with a thin smile, "I wonder if you could give me a hand?"

"We can try," Lee said, smiling brightly and twirling his beads, "It's a bit public here, but what the hell, I have always attempted to be a friend to man."

"Oh, wonderful," the dark stranger said, looking both pleased and relieved. "I've had such a hard time finding what I need. I'm a scholar, you see, and just at the moment I am looking for Bizarre Genitals and Outrageous Sex Practices."

"And they sent you to us?" Drag Thing asked, surprised. It was certainly the oddest approach she had ever heard of. And so direct. Whatever had happened to romance?

"The woman at the Information desk assured me that you would be able to take care of me here," he said.

"We are but strangers in a strange land," Drag Thing said, smiling coyly. She wasn't altogether sure just what her own personal practices were, her memory on that score was muddled, but in any case she was not much inclined to share them with strangers. Still, in the interests of scholarship....

Lee, however, was less reluctant. "Exactly how outrageous did you have in mind?" he asked, batting his eyelashes. It wasn't, after all, as if he hadn't some stories to tell, though he had not realized that his reputation had gotten quite that far afield. He had a good mind who was spreading those tales, too: his friend, Jay. He'd settle that bucket mouth's gander for him when next they met!

"I'm sorry," the gentleman said, adjusting his spectacles on his nose and peering at them intently, "But I think I am perhaps a bit confused?"

"You're confused? We are the ones whose private portions have been publicly sullied," Drag Thing said with a haughty sniff. "I don't know how you would like it if someone questioned your qualifications."

"Frankly, I don't see where my qualifications come into it," the gentleman said, "But I am Professor I.E. Dismal, and I am a serious scientist doing major research, and if you want to know, I have the Bakersfield Beaver behind me."

"And the Fresno fishworm up front, it looks like to me," Lee said, glancing down meaningfully. He was well experienced in sizing things up. "You're not exactly *Playgirl* material, you know, although I for one have no interest in your beaver, or how it got its pet name, for that matter, but I can pretty well imagine."

"No more interested am I," Drag Thing agreed, and I can't see how with qualifications like those you can feel free to insult our lovely selves."

"Look, this is going nowhere," Professor Dismal said impatiently. "I want what I want, I tell you. Either you have Bizarre Genitals, or you do not, and I haven't the time to play games. Now which is it?"

"There are some games," Lee said, "that a girl doesn't consider proper to play with a stranger without at least a little preamble. Now, if you would like a teensy kiss…." He puckered his lips and leaned forward.

Professor Dismal fairly leaped backward and regarded her askance. "Never mind," he said quickly, "I'll look for that elsewhere. Just tell me if you can help me with New Found Fun in a Cardboard Box? I'm looking for that, too."

"Oh, right," Lee said with a giggle and a quick flip of his wrist, "And I suppose if we fall for that one, you'll be asking for paper tits next."

Drag Thing guffawed. Professor Dismal fled, shaking his head in exasperation.

CHAPTER THIRTEEN

"That damned cat clawed me half to death," Caleb mumbled. He felt weird, like he was drunk or something. And feverish. His head buzzed like a stirred-up hornet's nest. "I hope you killed that fucker."

"I know I wounded her, for sure," Lawrence said. "But she ran off. In that crowd, I couldn't get another shot."

"What if she comes after me again?" Caleb struggled to look over his shoulder, as if expecting She Cat to appear in the corridor behind them. "That monster hates me. She wants to kill me."

They were back at the Wald Med Building, the Castro and their encounter with Jackle and Hyde far behind them, but he still didn't feel safe. As big as that cat was, she could probably get from there to here in a couple of leaps, at least to his muddled way of thinking. If only his head wasn't so fuzzy.

"Don't worry about that," Sylvester said. "You'll be safe here. You've got the three of us to look after you, don't forget."

"Is that supposed to make me feel better?" Caleb said, in a voice dripping scorn. "You didn't keep that cat off my neck before, did you?"

"Well, really, she did take us by surprise," Sylvester said. "Anyway, at least we got you out of that mob before the police got hold of you. Think how that would look on the evening news, you covered in feathers, trying to explain how you had been clawed half to death by a rampaging pussycat. Here we are." He opened the door to Caleb's private quarters. "You just rest here for a while, take it easy. Shall we get you something to drink? A beer, maybe?"

151

Caleb stumbled inside, flashing briefly on the beers he had served them. "No, I don't want anything. I just want to be left alone for a while," he said. "I need to lie down. Give me an hour or two. I'll be all right once I've had a nap."

"You want me to help you clean up?" Curly asked. "I can get those things off you and tuck you into bed, if you want."

Caleb thought he detected an oddly hopeful note in his voice. *Crap, just what I need*, he told himself with a mental groan, *a fag Homeland agent trying to pluck my feathers*.

"No, I'm fine," he said curtly, and closed the door firmly after himself. He started to waddle toward the bathroom, but the room began to spin violently around him. He changed direction and made it to the sofa in the nick of time, collapsing face down on it. He felt like he was on fire, like he was burning up.

In a minute, he was out cold.

* * * * * * *

"I'm hungry," Curly said. "All that excitement worked up an appetite."

"There's a steak joint down the street," Lawrence said. "Come on, I'll treat you to a big piece of meat."

Pffft, poof, Curly replied noisily.

Sylvester puckered his lips, which produced yet another explosion from Curly.

Lawrence laughed. "Want to come with us?" he asked Sylvester. "I'll bet a good thick juicy one would do you some good too."

"Thanks but no thanks," Sylvester said. "I don't think I have much appetite." He sniffed the fumes wafting about his head.

"Suit yourself. Come on, Curly." The two of them strolled down the corridor to the elevator.

Sylvester watched them go, waiting until the elevator door had closed after them. Then he went quickly down the hall in the opposite direction and let himself into his own apartment and breathed a great sigh of relief.

What an exercise in folly the evening had been! Really, between that egocentric fool, Caleb Wald, and those two morons who had been assigned to him, he was lucky they had not all ended up under arrest, which would have been a real embarrassment to the president.

As it was, for all their efforts they had accomplished nothing but wasted time. Drag Thing was still at large, and so was Doctor Jackle, and to make things worse, they had lost their hostage, Melissa Hyde. Everything had gone wrong. And on top of everything else, his nerves were all on edge. He badly needed to relax.

Fortunately, he had exercised his usual brilliant foresight. He had paid a visit to Chinatown just that afternoon, where he had early on found the purveyor he wanted, and he was well prepared now to relieve his tension in his favorite way.

He went directly to his closet and flung the door open. There was a flurry of movement on the floor. He looked down and smiled happily, already feeling a growing warmth in his loins as he anticipated what was to come.

"Hello, girls," he said, beaming, "I promised you I wouldn't be late."

* * * * * * *

"Good steaks, huh?" Lawrence asked as they returned to the Wald Med building a bit later.

"Mine was delish," Curly agreed. "But I sure wish we could find that beer Wald gave us the other night."

"Yeah, that was different," Lawrence agreed. "It had a nice nose."

"A nose? On a beer?"

"That's gourmet talk," Lawrence said. "That's how they describe beers to one another, the famous drinkers."

"Gee, you know everything, don't you?" Curly said in awe.

"It was definitely fruity," Lawrence added, warming to his subject in the glow of his companion's adulation.

"I like fruity," Curly agreed enthusiastically.

"With lots of acid."

"Plus, its nose tasted good, too, in my opinion," Curly said, smiling in memory; but his smile quickly faded. "Except, no one seems to know that brand. Yellow River, wasn't that what he said it was called?"

"Yes. He said it was Chinese, didn't he? We'll have to look at some of the specialty stores, someplace where the Asiatics hang out, like down in Japantown, maybe," Lawrence said. They stepped out of the elevator on their floor. "I suppose we should check in with Sylvester before we call it a night, make sure he's okay."

"He looked a little peaked, didn't he?" Curly agreed.

They came down the corridor to the green painted door of Sylvester's room. It was closed. They paused outside it. Lawrence lifted a hand to knock and hesitated.

"Maybe he's asleep by now," Curly said in a whisper.

"No, I don't think so," Lawrence said. He could hear a murmur of voices from beyond the green door—a television, its volume turned low. He knocked softly. "Sylvester?" he called.

"Go away," Sylvester's voice ordered them from within. "I am conducting an interrogation."

"Interrogation? We're supposed to be in on it when you do one of those," Lawrence called back. "You know what the manual says: you aren't supposed to do an interrogation alone. No one-on-one torture, it's very specific."

He shoved at the door. It swung open to reveal a startled looking Sylvester, sitting in a dark leather desk chair. His suit coat was draped over his lap. A large white hen sat atop the desk. She blinked at the two newcomers, fluttered her wings nervously and said, "Brawck." Behind her, images flitted on a television screen. A couple jounced and jiggled energetically atop a bed with dirty sheets.

"You're interrogating a chicken?" Curly asked, puzzled.

Sylvester's suit coat jiggled on his lap. Lawrence strode quickly across the room and snatched it away. "Shit. No, he's fucking a chicken," he said.

Curly frowned. "Isn't that against the rules of interrogation?" he said. "No sex, the way I remember the lessons. They totally emphasized that part, didn't they? No sex with

154

the individual being interrogated. Branding irons, yes. Sex, no."

He scratched his shiny scalp and looked at Lawrence. "Only, I don't remember if they specifically said chickens. I'd have to check the manual on that one. Where would you brand a chicken, anyway?"

"Get out," Sylvester cried, his voice breaking into a near falsetto. "Get out of here, you imbeciles." He tossed the chicken to the floor. She stumbled around dazedly in a wide circle, flapping her wings and clucking indignantly. "We are watching a soap opera together."

"What? All My Chickens?" Lawrence laughed and wagged an admonishing finger under Sylvester's nose. "You know what I think, Sylvester, my boy? I think you're the one who's going to get out. And I mean *out*, if you follow me."

Sylvester turned pale. He jumped to his feet and struggled to tug his trousers up and get them closed. "You wouldn't tell, would you?" he asked on a note of pleading. "Tell the agency, I mean. We were just having a little innocent fun, my friends and me. It doesn't mean anything, not anything serious. It was all innocent, I swear it."

"Those chickens were virgins, I'll bet, "Lawrence said. "You call that innocent fun, you roisterous rooster, you?"

"Look, we're partners, the three of us," Sylvester said in a pleading voice. "We're all in this together, right? Remember our motto, Homeland, Homeland, over all, Homeland, Homeland Forever."

"We're not that kind of partners, not in chicken-cocking we're not," Lawrence said in a scolding voice. "Look, Syl, tell you what, here's an offer you can't refuse. We'll keep our mouths zipped up," he made a zipping motion with his fingers, "and you resign from the agency. Immediately. You can say something came up." He pointed at Sylvester's dwindling penis, just disappearing inside his trousers. "Just tell them it was a little problem. Real little, but you don't have to say that. That part of it can stay between the three of us. And the chickens."

"Bastards," Sylvester said, fastening his belt. He started to pick up the hen atop the desk.

"And leave the chickens," Lawrence said. "We may need them as witnesses."

Sylvester snatched his jacket out of Lawrence's hand and stormed from the room with as much dignity as he could muster under the circumstances. A minute later they heard the door of the elevator whoosh open and closed.

Lawrence burst into a fit of laughter. He slapped Curly on the back. "Dumb fucker," he said. "I never could stand the guy."

"He was pretty cold, I thought," Curly said.

"Well, we're done with him now, and good riddance, I say."

"Do you think he'll really resign?"

"For sure," Lawrence said. "He wouldn't want us turning in a report saying we caught him diddling Henny Penny, would he? I'm pretty sure that's not sanctioned by Homeland. He'd not only be canned, he'd be the joke of the agency."

Curly looked at the two hens. "Uh, speaking of the chickens, what are we going to do with them?" he asked.

Lawrence looked at them too and grinned. "Hey, there's two of them, isn't there?" he said, "And there's two of us. Know what I mean?" He nudged Curly in the ribs with an elbow.

"What? You mean, cook them?"

Lawrence laughed. "You are so cute, you know that? Hell, I mean, we fuck them. You saw that little pee-pee of Sylvester's. These babies aren't even half broken in yet. I'll bet the one on the desk still has her little chicken cherry."

"Gee, I don't know." Curly looked solemnly at the hen. She tilted her head and blinked at him appraisingly. "I never did it with a chicken before."

Lawrence lifted the chicken up and turned her backside toward Curly. "Now, what does that remind you of?" he asked.

Curly's eyes went wide. *Kaboom* went a voluminous fart. "It looks like Sylvester's mouth," he said, "When he's all prissy like."

"Good boy," Lawrence said, giving him a pat on the shoulder. "So, all you do is, you pretend it's the dickhead

156

gobbling the goop. Think of that, old Sylvester wetting your whanger."

At that suggestion, Curly looked down and fluttered his lashes shyly. Lawrence noticed how long and thick his lashes were, like a little boy's. God, this guy was such a baby-doll, he thought with a happy grin.

"Did you ever—you know—with a chicken?" Curly asked in a shy stammer.

"Me?" Lawrence gave a raucous laugh. "Shit yes. I grew up on a farm. All the boys did it with the animals, except for the guys that were queer. Hell, I bet you couldn't think of an animal I haven't poked. Go ahead, try me. Name an animal."

Curly thought for a moment. "A llama?" he suggested. He had seen a couple of them once at a petting zoo and had thought they were real cute, although up till now he had never thought of them in a sexual context. He was certainly broadening his education since he had teamed up with Lawrence.

"Well," Lawrence said after a moment's consideration, "I fooled around with a Catholic priest when I was a kid, but hell, everybody did that, it was kind of an after school gig, like Four-H, you know, or band practice. What I meant was, a four-legged animal. Like a sheep. Sheep are great. And pigs. Pigs are pretty good too, but they smell kind of funny."

"Did you ever do it with a cow?" Curly found himself fascinated by his friend's level of sophistication. He realized how little experience he had really had—mostly with his own self up till he had met Lawrence.

But he had thought about cows sometimes because, when you looked at them, like the time he visited his uncle's farm, everything was kind of, well, right there in front of you, like you couldn't not notice it. He had never told anybody before, but it did kind of turn him on. He just had never realized till now that it was normal. It certainly proved that he wasn't queer, didn't it, regardless of him and Lawrence fooling around together?

"Oh, sure," Lawrence said. "Cows are kind of tricky, though. I mean, with a sheep, say, or a pig, you've got plenty of time for the romance stuff, you know, you can kind of take your time, make a real session of it, sweet talk and all, they like that stuff. Especially the sheep. But cows, now, they are strictly business women, they like it in one quick poke, wham bam thank you ma'am kind of thing. So what you got to do, see, is you put the cow in a stall, face in, of course, and you get a step stool and you put it behind the cow so you can get to her in a hurry when you're ready, see, and then you go to work yourself up till you're just about there and then you run up the stool and shove it home. And the milk is delivered, so to speak."

"Gosh. You've done it all, haven't you?" Curly's admiration was evident in his voice.

Lawrence grinned modestly. "Well, let's just say I have been to the rodeo a time or two. And then some. So what do you say, old buddy, we have ourselves a little party? Anyway, I'll give you a hand getting started." He reached for the front of Curly's trousers.

"Lawrence...."

"Call me Larry," he said in a romantic whisper.

One of the hens said, "Brawck."

* * * * * * *

Caleb felt weird when he regained consciousness, really weird. He had fallen asleep on the sofa in his office, passed out, in fact, still dressed in his full owl regalia. He woke up with a drove of bees going wild in his head and his mouth as dry as the Sahara. For a moment, he couldn't think where he was, or how he had gotten there.

He stumbled to the kitchen and got himself a cold can of Coca Cola from the refrigerator, popped the top, and drank half of it down greedily. He felt like he had a fever, but when he put his hand to his forehead, it felt normal.

Maybe, he thought, *I got infected when that damn wild cat clawed me.* He glanced down at his arm. To his surprise, the claw marks had faded almost entirely. It took a minute more for something else to register in his mind. His arm was not his arm—at least, it was not the arm he used to have. This arm was enormous and positively bulging with muscle.

He set the Coke aside and went into the bathroom and looked at himself in the mirror. The scratches on his face were nearly healed up as well, but that wasn't what arrested his attention. Either the mirror was hanging lower than it had been before, or he was taller than he was. He actually had to stoop down to look at his reflection.

Alarmed, he turned to leave the bathroom and in his excitement, he grabbed at the door too energetically. To his astonishment, the door ripped free of its hinges, wood splintering noisily.

Jesus H. Christ, I barely tugged at it, he thought, flabbergasted by his newfound strength. He looked down at his hand, flexing his fingers and staring at them. His hand was twice the size it had been before. It was the size of a catcher's mitt. He looked again at the muscles bulging in his arm.

I'm strong, he told himself. *I am enormous and strong, super strong.*

In an instant, the explanation came to him: it was the damned cat, and the scratches she left on him. That had to be the cause. Over the months while he had spied on the Alley Thing project, he had watched the cat balloon in size and grow more aggressive, and demonstrably stronger.

Now it had happened to him, too. He had turned into someone—*some thing*—else. The realization staggered his imagination. For starters, it meant that Alley Thing was a success. If only they could get hold of Janet Jackle, or Melissa Hyde, and get the formula from them—his fortune would be made. He could think of a score of ways this could be turned into pure gold by a man with his smarts.

But that was in the future. For the moment, there were the changes in himself to consider. He could not yet think what it all meant, but one thing was certain: he was powerful, super strong. He had never been an ordinary man, if you were to be honest, but now he truly was extraordinary.

Probably, he could do all sorts of things, too, maybe even fly. He flapped his wings expectantly, but his feet remained rooted to the floor. Well, maybe he would have to work on that some, he thought, though he wasn't ready to rule out the possibility till he had tried it further. Anyway, the point was, he was unquestionably something else now, something like Superman or Spiderman, one of the comic book heroes. He paused to think. *But what, exactly? Or rather, who?*

The Owl. The thought popped into his mind. That was it. He wasn't Superman, and he wasn't Spiderman, but he was no longer just Caleb Wald, handsome stud about town, either. He was…it flashed on and off in his mind as if written in neon, yellow and green: *I am The Owl.*

His head hurt, though, now that he had gotten past the first few minutes of surprise. And he felt dizzy to boot. He tried to walk across the office and bumped into his desk, caromed off of that and staggered into the wall, knocking a picture of himself loose from its hanger. It fell to the floor with a crash of breaking glass.

Shit. A lot of good it was going to do him to turn into Super Bird if he couldn't even walk straight. He needed practice—and maybe a different set of bird feet. He'd have to talk to that woman….

He opened the office door, more carefully this time, and went out into the hall, vaguely intending to take the elevator down to the lobby and get himself some air—to try to clear his head—but in the hall, he heard sounds from one of the lab rooms, and paused, listening.

Yes. There it was again: boyish giggles, and something else, too, it sounded like a squawk. Like—but this made no sense—it sounded like a chicken croaking heatedly. *Cluck, brawck, cluck.* Yes, it was definitely a chicken, and definitely in a state of excitement.

He approached the closed door on padded owl-feet, walking carefully now, making no sound beyond the whispering rustle of his tail feathers as they brushed to and fro. Cautiously, being mindful of his newfound strength, he inched the door open.

His eyes flew wide in astonishment at the scene before him and despite his intention to employ stealth, he gasped aloud. It was those two Homeland Security agents, Lawrence and Curly, and they were…they were…his mind refused even to form the words—and they were doing it with chickens! His fine feathered friends. Practically members of his avian family…his goddamn little sisters, if you wanted to

160

look at it like that, and here they were, being violated by these two fiends!

"You fowl fuckers," he roared angrily, "Avian abusers! Poultry pederasts!"

The two men looked up, startled, in his direction. The chickens blinked, and one of them cried loudly, "Barraawk! Barraawk!"

With a shriek of rage, Caleb threw the door wide with a thunderous bang, wood splintering, and leaped into the room, his tail bobbing, owl-wings flapping furiously. Feathers flew.

CHAPTER FOURTEEN

"Honey? Peter?" Teri let herself in their front door and closed it quietly behind her. There was a faint groan from the living room. She flipped on the ceiling light as she went in

Peter blinked and sat up on the couch, naked. "Mmpf," he grunted. "What time is it?"

"About four A.M.," she said. "Are you okay?"

"I've got a headache," he mumbled. He had the godfather of all headaches, actually. He got up and stumbled in the direction of the kitchen. "And my throat feels like sandpaper," he said. He filled a glass from the faucet and drained it, and filled it again.

Teri paused to take off her gun and holster and toss them on a chair before she followed him. She watched him from the kitchen doorway. "Did you make it to the Castro tonight?" she asked.

Sipping his second glass of water more decorously, Peter took a minute to consider that. He must have, hadn't he? He vaguely remembered being with Lee—and crowds of people in funny costumes, and there was this giant owl....

"Yes," he said. "Of course I did."

"I didn't see you there," she said.

"Oh, you know how those mob things are," he said, turning toward her. "You could be three feet away from someone and not get a glimpse of them. Did you have any trouble?"

"Just one dust up, with some gangbangers," she said. "Oddly, they were the same ones I told you about before, remember, they had that brush in with Drag Thing a few nights ago. They call themselves The Moes. You didn't happen to see them while you were there, did you?"

162

He considered that for a moment. "No, I didn't. What happened? Did they make trouble?" he asked, glad to deflect attention even briefly from himself, at least until he had a chance to collect his thoughts. The mention of Drag Thing had made him uncomfortable.

"The Moes? I'll say. It was totally crazy, really. They were staging, like, some kind of live sex show right there on the sidewalk, with one of the guys taking on a whole pack of dogs. Can you imagine that? It was totally disgusting. And at the same time, one of them was trying to pimp this little gay boy."

"It certainly sounds bizarre," Peter said.

"It was, you can't imagine it," Teri agreed. "Anyway, the pimp resisted arrest and he managed to get hold of Jake's revolver and fired it into the crowd before we got him subdued. Unfortunately, I had to see to another disturbance and by that time the other two had gotten away. We've got the one, though, he seemed to be the ringleader, and with all the charges, attempted murder and prostitution and the live sex show, he'll be out of circulation for a long while."

"That's good news," he said. "I remember those boys now." A peculiar expression drifted over his face and his voice changed subtly. "They were very naughty, those three. The ringleader especially, Mister Moe. Naughty, naughty."

"Peter," Teri began, giving him a puzzled look—he seemed peculiar suddenly. But before she could say what was on her mind, the living room door suddenly crashed open, and Janet Jackle burst into the room with a mighty leap.

"Uh oh," Teri said, and ran for the chair where she had left her gun, but Janet, with her incredibly long legs, got there before her in two quick strides.

"Easy, now," Janet said, snatching Teri's gun off the chair and brandishing it. "Just do as I say, and no one will get hurt."

"Who are you?" Teri demanded.

"I'm Doctor Janet Jackle," the intruder said. "Don't you remember me?" She gave a coarse laugh—a cackle, really.

Teri stared at her. Janet Jackle? That was the woman who had attacked Caleb Wald outside the Copa Club the other night—but this wasn't her, surely. This nightmarish apparition was eight feet tall, maybe taller…only…Teri stared hard at her. There was a resemblance…it was like remembering someone from a dream. It was all so unreal. Teri shook her head. She didn't know what to make of it. Everything was so confusing.

"What are you doing here?" she asked instead. "What do you want?"

"I want Drag Thing," Janet said.

"Drag Thing?" Teri said, more bewildered than ever. "Why are you looking for him here?"

"Uh, what makes you think we would know anything about Drag Thing?" Peter asked.

"I saw the lady cop let him go earlier, in the Castro," Janet said, "And I got suspicious, so I followed her back here, and hung around outside to watch, and I saw Drag Thing climbing the fire escape to the roof, so I know he's in the building somewhere. And I put two and two together, and this is the logical place. Where are you hiding him?"

Teri laughed. "You think we've got Drag Thing stashed under the bed? Go ahead, take a look around, why don't you? She's a big girl, it would be kind of hard to hide her, don't you think?"

Janet looked around the room. The cop lady was right: it would be nearly impossible to hide that monstrosity anywhere. She went to open a closet door anyway and took a cursory glance inside, but without much hope. Nothing there but dresses—incredibly tacky dresses.

There was nothing in the bathroom, either, or the bedroom. There just was no place that would conceal someone as enormous as Drag Thing. She paused, scratching her head in puzzlement. Grimalkin approached to give her a measuring look, and sniffed and strolled away, disinterested.

Seeing the cat, Janet gave an anguished sob. "Oh, what a beautiful pussy you are, you are, what a beautiful pussy you are," she cried.

"Grimalkin?" Teri said. "He's a very friendly cat. You can pet him, if you want."

164

"What I want is Drag Thing," Janet snarled. "If he's not here, then he must still be on the roof. Come on, we'll go there." She waved the gun in the direction of the open door.

"But why do you need us?" Teri asked.

"I may need bargaining chips," Janet said. "And for crap's sake, you put on some pants," she snapped at the still naked Peter, "I don't want to have to watch your dingus flopping about like that. It's disgusting."

"There's nothing disgusting about my Peter," Teri said shortly.

"It's okay," Peter said. "It's probably kind of chilly on the roof anyway at this hour of the night." He found his robe and quickly slipped into it.

"Let's go," Janet said impatiently. She shepherded them out the door and down the hall toward the elevator. Teri kept one eye on the gun, watching for an opportunity to try to wrest it away from her, but Jackle was too careful to keep them at a distance and the gun trained on them.

The door to the Kravitz's apartment swung open as they neared it and Gladys Kravitz appeared in the open doorway, a suitcase in her hand.

"I don't care how you explain it," she said over her shoulder in an indignant voice. "I saw what I saw, Abner. That man with the shaved head had his hand up—well, I'm not going to say it aloud, but you know where he had it."

"I've told you and told you, he was looking for something," Abner said from inside the apartment.

"A cheap homosexual thrill, I should say. And I didn't see you struggling, if I may say so."

"This was a matter of national security," Abner said.

"Right," she fired back. "Like the president cares about your bodily functions. We have suppositories in the bathroom, you know."

"This was dynamite."

"They're very powerful suppositories!"

"He was a Homeland Security agent, Gladys. You have to let a Homeland agent do what he wants to you, it's the law. It wasn't like he was doing it for fun."

"He seemed to be enjoying himself well enough."

"He thought I had a stick of dynamite stashed there and he was looking for it. I've explained that a dozen times. He apologized after he'd had himself a thorough search. I was just cooperating, is all. I swear to you, I didn't enjoy it at all, honest, and I'll bet he didn't either. You can't blame a man for being thorough. Not when it's Homeland Security."

"Very thorough, it looked like to me." She gave a muffled sob. "Oh, Abner, what you've done is bad enough, please don't make it worse with feeble excuses. A stick of dynamite? And that Lee Appel person put it there, I suppose. And what was he doing in our apartment anyway, I'd like to know? With an eight foot drag queen. They told me quite plainly they were here to visit you. Are you trying to tell me you didn't invite them? For a little private party? A round or two of 'Lets-hide-the-dynamite,' perhaps? I'm a registered nurse, remember, a professional? I've heard all about this sort of disgusting nonsense, let me tell you. We get it in ER all the time. Vibrators and cucumbers and candles—but dynamite is a new one, I'll have to say. I'll give you credit for originality, at least."

She stepped into the hall, and found herself suddenly face to face with Janet Jackle. Gladys let out a bloodcurdling shriek. "Abner, Abner, it's the woman with the pussy," she screamed. "And she's got no pussy."

"Gladys," Abner started to say, but Gladys was gone. She dropped her suitcase and galloped down the hallway at a furious pace, screaming repeatedly and loudly. They heard her footsteps pounding down the stairs.

"I'm never coming back, Abner," she shouted as she fled. "You can play hide the stick with all the men in the world, for all I care."

"A nervous type, I'd say," Janet commented dryly as the footsteps faded into the distance.

"Gladys is a bit high strung," Peter said.

The elevator arrived and the door swished open. "Listen, Doctor Jackle," Teri tried to say, but Janet cut her off.

"Save it," she snapped, motioning them into the car. "Get in. We've got a Drag Thing to find."

They took the elevator up and emerged into the darkness of the roof, a gloom alleviated only slightly by the faint light of the moon struggling through the nighttime fog.

"Over there," Janet said, pointing them to a shadowy stretch against the wall of an abutting building—the most likely place for anyone to hide. She followed them, but there was no sign of Drag Queen in the darkness.

All at once Peter staggered and put a hand to his head, and gasped. "Oh, golly," he said.

"Peter, what's wrong?" Teri asked anxiously, putting an arm about him.

He groaned. "I feel dizzy all of a sudden," he muttered, leaning heavily against her.

"Spare me any tricks," Jackle said. She looked around in frustration. She had seen Drag Thing climbing up the fire escape no more than half an hour ago. He had to be here. But where?

"Wait here," she told Teri and Peter, "And no funny business." She returned to the patch of moonlight, peering behind some empty crates that had been abandoned, probably years earlier.

"I'm okay," Peter told Teri. He moved away from her and leaned heavily against the dusty brick wall.

He didn't look okay, though, to Teri's thinking. And he was breathing heavily, practically panting. She looked away from him and stared after Doctor Jackle, and wondered briefly if they could get to the elevator before she spotted them.

Peter was ill, though, she doubted he could move fast. Plus, Janet Jackle had the gun, and she looked insane. There was no telling what she might do. Teri was in great shape, but she had serious doubts about getting into a physical tussle with Janet Jackle. She was the biggest woman Teri had ever seen, too, if you discounted Drag Thing—she was scarcely recognizable as the same woman she'd met before. And that hair, like a tangle of copper wiring. What had happened to change her so?

Janet circled the roof slowly. There were any number of places where someone might hide, though most of them did not look as if they could conceal anyone as large as Drag

Thing. She had to be here, though. She had definitely come up the fire escape, and if she hadn't gone downstairs, then where was she?

"Oh, Doctor Jackle," a strange voice called from the gloom where she had left her hostages. "Yoo hoo."

"Who's there?" Janet demanded, whirling about in the direction of the voice. "Is that you, Drag Thing?"

Before she got an answer, however, a different voice said from the opposite side of the roof, "So, it is you, Doctor Jackle. I didn't recognize you before, but I ought to have known. It was Alley Thing, wasn't it, that changed you so? You took the formula."

Janet whirled in that direction, to see a strange apparition step into view—no, it didn't step so much as hop into view, like a bird walking, an eight foot tall goose with dingy white wings and feathers, and enormous yellow bird-feet.

"Who are you?" Janet demanded, staring at him. The feathers, the wings, the yellow bird feet—it looked like the costume Caleb Wald had worn in the Castro earlier in the evening, but this strange creature was twice Wald's size. Even his beak was bigger, monstrous in fact.

His laughter came out sounding like, "Hoo, Hoo. Don't you recognize me, you silly dyke?" he asked.

She peered closer. "It...it is you," she gasped. "Caleb Wald. But what happened to you? And why are dressed like a goose, with that enormous beak?"

"It is not a beak, and I am not a goose," he shouted angrily. I am...." He paused for dramatic effect and spread his wings to their fullest. "I am The Owl."

"The formula," Janet said in a burst of understanding. "Oh, yes, I get it, Alley Thing—but, how? I destroyed it all."

"The cat," he said. "That evil She Cat of yours. It was her claws. She scratched me when she attacked me in the Castro, and her claws infected me. I owe you for those scratches, dear Doctor Jackle. The beast might have killed me."

"And I owe you, too," she started to say, but she was interrupted.

168

"Oh, it's the naughty man again," Drag Thing said, sashaying out of the blackness at the other end of the roof. Teri trailed after her, looking completely bewildered.

"What—what happened to Peter?" Teri demanded. "He's vanished, and you...where did you come from? I didn't see...."

"So, Drag Thing," Janet Jackle said with a triumphant cackle, "We meet again, and this time you won't escape me, you bitch." She raised the gun and pointed it at Drag Thing. "I vowed to my darling Melissa that I would kill you for what you did to her. Thanks to you, she lies now in a coma...."

"It was not Drag Thing who did that to her," Drag Thing said indignantly, hands on hips. "Drag Thing does not assault women, she rescues them, from naughty men." She lifted one hand and pointed a beer bottle sized finger at Caleb Wald, "Drag Thing rescued your friend from *that* naughty man right there. He was hitting her."

"Aha, I was right to begin with," Janet cried, instinctively recognizing the truth of what she'd just heard. In her heart, she had known all along that Caleb must somehow be to blame. "Wald, you bastard, I should have...."

She started to turn the gun in The Owl's direction, but she was not quick enough. He lashed out with one great feathered wing and knocked the gun from her hand. It clattered to the rooftop and vanished into the darkness.

"Yes it was me who sent your bitch girlfriend to La-La Land. I should have put you into a coma, instead," The Owl said, "But it's not too late yet to correct my mistake."

In one mighty hop, he leaped across the space separating them and seized Janet by the throat, choking her violently. She gasped and struggled, and managed to break free of his deadly grip, but when she pulled away from him, she tripped on one of his chicken-feet and fell to the rooftop, hitting her head hard. The blow stunned her. A kaleidoscope of stars exploded before her eyes.

The Owl lifted one webbed foot, intending to deliver a vicious kick to Janet's head, but Drag Thing intervened. She took two giant steps forward and smacked The Owl mightily alongside his tufted crown.

"Stop that, I say, you naughty, naughty man," she ordered.

"You fucking fruitcake, I should have killed you when I had the chance," The Owl cried. Forgetting Janet Jackle for the moment, he threw himself instead at Drag Thing and they began to wrestle violently, stumbling this way and that.

At first, it seemed as if Drag Thing had the upper hand, but to her surprise and dismay, she suddenly found herself beginning to tire. A moment or two before she had felt as strong as Super Woman, and now, her strength was rapidly fading. She was growing weaker by the moment. She could see that she was no longer a match for this avian evil. Great Dame Edna, what was she to do? She struggled to find some advantage, some weakness in The Owl's frightening strength.

They staggered close to the edge of the roof. Teri could see that The Owl was getting the better of the match. Without quite understanding why, she had an odd sense that she must help Drag Thing, and she began to search in the darkness for the fallen gun. Nearby, Janet sat up, shaking her head dazedly.

"The Owl is overpowering Drag Thing," Teri said, "We've got to save her. Help me, please."

Drag Thing's strength was definitely abandoning her. She suddenly realized what was happening: she was changing again, turning back, into…she didn't know what, exactly, someone other than herself. And The Owl was so strong. Drag Thing sank to her knees, The Owl's hands at her throat. She felt herself pulled, dragged toward the edge of the roof.

"Let's see if the Tinker Bell can fly," The Owl said. He shoved Drag Thing halfway over the edge of the roof. Dangling in the air, Drag Thing sought desperately for something to hold onto, to save herself from being thrown to the street ten stories below, but her grasping hands could find nothing. The Owl bent over her, tugging at her shoulders. Drag Thing felt so weak…she was helpless to save herself. Another moment, and….

There was a sudden roar and something flew through the dim moonlight and with a powerful leap, landed on The Owl's back.

170

"Missy Hyde," Janet cried, scrambling to her feet and running toward them.

The force of the giant cat's leap sent The Owl tumbling over Drag Thing, and into empty space. He and the cat seemed almost to linger suspended in the air for a moment, clinging to one another, and then they fell. The Cat emitted a sound suspiciously like a yowl of triumph and The Owl gave a screech of horror. As he fell, he flapped his wings vainly, hoping at the last that perhaps he really could fly.

* * * * * * *

Ten stories below, a weeping Gladys Kravitz had just told a repentant Abner she forgave him. "But, Abner," she added sternly, "absolutely, no more dynamite sticks, I don't care where they're hidden."

"Gladys, I swear to you," he said in a solemn voice, crossing his heart, "If such a thought ever crosses my mind again, may a ton of bricks fall from the sky upon me."

* * * * * * *

"Missy Hyde," Janet screamed, but Owl and Pussycat were both gone.

Teri ran to the roof's edge. It was not Drag Thing dangling there, in imminent danger of falling as well, but her beloved Peter.

"Peter, my darling," she sobbed, dragging him back to the safety of the roof.

"Teri," he gasped. He scrambled over the parapet and fainted dead away.

"It's all right, honey, it's okay," Teri crooned, cradling him in her arms. It wasn't until minutes later that she realized Janet Jackle had gone, vanishing into the night.

CHAPTER FIFTEEN

Melissa was still weak, but she was conscious. Janet held her in a fierce embrace, and told her everything that had happened since she had fallen into her coma.

"And now I am trapped," Janet concluded, "In the body of a freak."

"But not forever, my darling," Melissa said. "We'll go away together, some place where we can be alone, away from the madding crowds, and I will work ceaselessly, until I have found an antidote to Alley Thing. I vow to you, just as you vowed to me—I will see that you are restored to your true self."

"But, in the meantime, look at me!" Janet practically wailed. I'm a monster. There's nothing that will make me look right. Not even Industrial Strength Oil of Olay would do it."

"Never mind, my love. I love you regardless. The most important thing is, we will be together."

"Forever?"

"Forever,' Melissa vowed.

They embraced happily.

"But we'll order a barrel or two of that Oil of Olay," Melissa said. "Just to be safe."

* * * * * * *

Larry and Curly had been hospitalized at Saint Maria Alfonso for two days when their chief, Karl Nuremberg, came to see them. Larry's first impression when he saw their boss come into their room was that it was really quite flattering that he had taken the trouble to come visit them in the hospital.

"Boys," Nuremberg greeted them, "How's it going?"

"Okay," Larry said, a little hesitantly. Looking at Karl's solemn face, Larry began to feel a trifle differently about their boss's arrival. Karl's expression was not at all friendly. It seemed less concerned than accusing. Larry had the distinct impression that this was about to turn into some kind of a trial.

"We're doing great," Curly said, oblivious as always to any nuances of mood.

Karl regarded them solemnly for an uncomfortably long moment, looking wordlessly from one to the other. To break the ominous silence, Larry said, "Food could be better."

"The Jell-O's good, though," Curly said. "And the chocolate pudding. I love chocolate pudding. With nuts."

"The food's not a problem," Karl said finally. "We're moving you out of this place, to a private facility upstate, one of our own. The medics should be here in a minute or two, and we've got an ambulance ready and waiting downstairs. It's about a forty-minute ride. If it's any consolation, they tell me the food is really great where you're going. No nuts, though. If you boys are smart, you'll forget you've got a taste for nuts, if you catch my drift. Plus this place is way out in the country. You don't have to worry about traffic noise or air pollution, any of that stuff." He paused. "Or, say, media attention. Nosy reporters, that sort of thing."

"Reporters?" Larry said.

"Reporters," Karl repeated. "Like the ones hanging around downstairs in the lobby when I came in. We'll be going out the back way, of course. Where they won't accost us. We've got a dozen agents keeping the freight elevator clear for us. We even requisitioned an ambulance off the street, put some guy with a cardiac business out, so there would be no record of this trip. And the driver is a free-lancer, a guy by the name of Luis. He needs money bad, seems he ran up some incredible expenses lately, and was having a hard time landing a gig, so we had no problem buying his silence. The point I'm making is, the agency is in full safety mode, thanks to you boys."

173

"Gee, it's great of the Agency to look after us like this," Curly said, beaming. He saw Larry's disapproving scowl and his own smile faded. "Isn't it?"

"We've put a total shut-down on any information here at the hospital. National security. Anybody breathes a word about you boys and your problems, they will be on their way to a vacation at Guantanamo; a long vacation, no tee shirts, no postcards. That shut down includes the two of you two, by the way. Once this conversation is ended, you will both of you forget it and everything that happened leading up to it. Totally everything," Karl emphasized.

"We won't say nothing to anybody," Larry assured him solemnly. "You don't have to worry about us."

"Our lips are sealed," Curly said. He did the zipper thing across his mouth.

"That's good," Karl said, "Because, as you know, the agency does not like to be embarrassed. Especially not now, with every pinko do-gooder and leftie reporter looking for blood. And you have got to admit, you guys are an embarrassment. Bombs up assholes. How is that going to look on the news? Not to mention this last dust up of yours."

"We got blind-sided on that one," Larry said defensively. "Caught off guard. No way we could have seen it coming."

"By an owl," Curly said. Larry shot him a fierce glance.

"An owl." Karl said it flatly, more of a statement than a question.

"Yes sir," Larry said quickly. "A man dressed as an owl, that is to say, not an actual owl. It was Halloween, you understand. Here in San Francisco they get real carried away at Halloween. A guy dressed like an owl wasn't all that unusual. There were walking hot dogs and hundreds of drag queens and a sailor with great, uh, sailor stuff. I even saw a watermelon. That owl person looked near normal compared to some."

"That must explain the feathers," Karl said. "I heard there were feathers everywhere when the paramedics came to get you."

"Yes sir." Larry said, "There were some feathers."

"They had to remove some from your backsides, the way I heard it," Karl said. "With tweezers. The nurses are still talking about that amongst themselves, downstairs in the cafeteria. I sat near them and drank some coffee and listened to what they had to say. It made quite a colorful little story, feathers in butt holes. They were laughing their heads off."

Uh, that owl guy sort of kicked us," Larry said.

"Besides, there were some chickens involved too, sir," Curly said. "A lot of the feathers came from the chickens."

"Chickens?" Nuremberg echoed, his expression increasingly grim.

"Two of them," Curly said, head bobbing. "White ones. Female hens."

"Hens?"

There was another lengthy silence. Curly squirmed around in his bed. Larry tried to shrink into his pillow.

"Let me ask you," Karl said finally, "Since you mentioned San Francisco and drag queens and the like, I mean, you are right, weird things do go on here, in this town, all kinds of things. What I am curious to know is, was there anything, you know, of a sexual nature in what happened to you boys?"

"No sir," both said at once, emphatically.

"The reason I ask is, it does look a little odd, don't you agree, the two of you in the hospital at the same time, and both of you with splints on your national symbols. You don't see that very often."

"He jumped on our laps, sir," Larry said. "The owl."

"Smashed the chickens," Curly said. "Just squished them flat. The one I was holding, she wasn't nothing but a pile of mush and feathers, it was awful, I...." He became aware of Larry glowering at him from the other bed and his voice trailed off. "It was simply dreadful," he said in a morose whisper.

Karl lifted the briefcase he was carrying and set it atop the bedside table and opened it. "I've brought resignations for the two of you to sign." He put up a hand before either of them could say anything. "Now, don't worry, we're not cutting you adrift. The agency takes care of its own, you know that, even when they have become an embarrassment. What

175

we have done, see, is the Chief made some calls to friends of his around the country, he went to a lot of personal trouble on your behalf, I hope you appreciate that.

"Anyhow, it seems like the Chicago Police Department can use a couple of extra officers. As soon as you are both recovered—and we do not want to hurry you on that, you can take all the time you need to get those things off of your flagpoles—as soon as you do, you will be reporting there for duty, to Chicago. I have got all the details written down here for you, everything cut and dry."

"Chicago's a nice town," Curly said. "I was there once. They got a big lake. Big as an ocean. Bigger, maybe."

"Will we be like, detectives? Homicide, maybe?" Larry asked hopefully, trying to put as brave a face as he could on what was happening.

"More like beat cops," Karl said, offering each of them a slip of paper and a ballpoint pen. "To start, anyway. But, who knows what the future holds for any of us? You do your jobs, make a good impression, you can always work your way up. Sign where I put the little red exes."

* * * * * * *

To his own surprise, Tom had found that he liked living at The Heartfelt Hands mission. He had never had a room of his own before. Even as a kid, he had shared a bedroom with four brothers and a sister; and he couldn't remember ever before having three squares a day either.

He was expected to work, of course. Father Flinnigan had made that clear from the beginning: "Everybody has a job to do," he put it. "Working hands are busy hands, that's our motto here at the mission."

Even that wasn't so bad, though. In Tom's case, the "work" mostly involved taking care of a couple of dozen dogs that were kenneled in the yard behind the house, and he had quickly discovered that he had a real affinity for the pooches, and they had welcomed him as one of their own. For the first time in his memory, he felt like he really belonged. Even with the Moes, he hadn't felt this welcomed into a group.

176

All in all, he figured he was one lucky dude, all things considered. It was true, from time to time he wondered about the others. The last he had seen, Hector was getting himself arrested, and most likely he was probably still in jail, but, hey, Hector had always been a mean shit, and knowing him, he would probably end up boss man wherever he got sent, so there wasn't much point in crying over him.

As for Archie, well, Archie was pretty good at looking out for Archie. They had run into each other briefly just the day before, and Archie had confessed that he was living in the Castro with a couple of drag queens.

"Betty and Veronica," he said. "You saw them, Halloween night, in the Castro."

Tom's memories of that night, however, were of another kind. The drag queens had faded from his mind.

It was funny, though, he had never figured Archie for anything kinky like that, like drag things. Just went to show, you never could tell about a guy. Of course, Archie had denied it when Tom asked if he was porking the queens—but he had that satisfied look about him, like a guy was getting it regular.

Tom had just shrugged it all off, though. The important things was, Archie had looked like he was happy, like he was doing just fine.

The same as me, Tom thought proudly.

"You know, Padre," he said to Father Flinnigan one morning while he was cleaning out the kennels, "This is the best thing that ever happened to me, finding you, The Heartfelt Hands, the dogs and all. I mean—hyuk, hyuk, hyuk—who'd have ever thought it: me, cleaned up and straight, working a regular job, doing something worthwhile. I owe it all to you."

"Well, no, you owe it all to yourself," Father Flinnigan said. "You were the one who made the decision to go straight."

"Course, it's not a regular job. I mean, I don't get paid, or anything." Tom looked wistful.

"Everybody has to start somewhere," Father Flinnigan said. "And, if you do your job well and prove yourself, we'll see about putting you on the payroll down the road. But, first

177

things first. How are you doing, so far? Getting along okay with the dogs, are you?"

"Great. I even got myself a special friend already, Willi," Tom said. "You know, that big old Great Dane you found in the Castro? Willi and me have gotten to be real pals."

"That's great. He's a very loveable dog," the father said.

"He sure is, really loveable," Tom agreed. "Plus, he's beautifully marked, as we say here at the shelter. Course, we had to clean that lavender stuff off his toenails. Looked too fruity, you know? I wouldn't want that in my buddy. I like my guy to look like a guy."

Father Flinnigan put a hand on Tom's shoulder. "Keep up the good work," he said. "And take good care of Willi."

"I promise," Tom said. "Besides, you want to know, I'm figuring Willi will take good care of me, too, once he gets to know me better. That's my plan."

"I'm glad to see that you really love the dogs," Father Flinnigan said.

"Oh, I do, I love every single one of them." Tom paused and grinned. "Hyuk, hyuk, hyuk. Of course, they say you never forget your first one."

When Father Flinnigan had walked away, Tom started thinking about the prospect of actually getting paid for his work. When he had a few bucks, he could afford the occasional present for Willi. He could just imagine how grateful Willi would be for a little pampering. Guys liked that shit.

* * * * * * *

Sylvester had already turned in his resignation, citing "personal matter" as his reason. He hoped that Lawrence and Curly stuck to their words and kept their mouths shut, but even if they talked, he was already gone from Homeland.

Not that the agency couldn't touch a private citizen, if they wanted to. That was the whole point of the agency, that no one was safe. Homeland could nail anyone, anywhere, anytime, no matter how innocent. It was the thing of which they were proudest: they made their own rules.

178

The truth was, however, and he faced it philosophically, it was time for him to be moving on. Luckily, he'd had the foresight to arrange for another identity way back when he had been working for the CIA, just in case. CIA agents who screwed up had the unfortunate habit of disappearing from sight. He had long ago reasoned that if he was going to disappear, it should be at his own time and of his own doing.

Which was exactly what he was going to do now, was already in the final stages of doing: disappearing. He had the works: a social security card, a driver's license, credit cards, even a passport. As of this day, Sylvester Katt had ceased to exist. He was now Harry Beaver.

He had been stashing away his money as well, so he had enough of a nest egg to take care of him for a while, though he didn't actually expect to have to live off of it. He had a plan for that, too. That was where he was different from putzes like Lawrence and Curly, who couldn't plan past their own noses.

He left the freeway at Petaluma. He had scoped out this place months earlier, as a precaution. He liked to be prepared, like in the Boy Scouts. He knew exactly where to find Cox's Chicken Ranch—"The World's Largest Chicken Ranch," as its sign proudly proclaimed alongside the highway, "Our eggs can't be beat!"

He drove through the open gate, up a short lane, and stopped in front of an enormous barn. He stepped out of Harry Beaver's brand new red Honda. The air was pungent with that smell peculiar to chicken farms: a heady blend of wet feathers and straw and chicken poop that took him back to his childhood in Tennessee. Fond memories assailed him.

A rooster crowed somewhere in the distance. A short, round man in bib overalls came out of the barn, saw Sylvester and walked toward him. "He'p you?" he asked politely, shoving a straw from one corner of his mouth to the other.

"I was looking for a job," Sylvester-now-Harry said. "Can you use any help?"

The man looked him up and down. Guy looked okay, except there was something funny about his mouth. *That mouth reminds me of somethin'*, Farmer Cox thought. *Can't 'zactly put my finger on it. It'll come to me, though.*

"Might could be I was," he said aloud, spitting out of the side of his mouth and passing the straw back again. "You had any 'sperience with poultry, son?"

"Lots," Harry said. "Chickens, turkey, ducks, geese— you name it, I guess I've fooled around with all of them at one time or another. Sometimes I feel like I have been married to poultry."

Farmer Cox chuckled and nodded knowingly. "Yep, times it can sure seem that way for a fella, can't it? Got mostly chickens here, you unnerstant. A duck or two from time to time, but mostly this is a chicken farm. That's why our name says, Cox's Chicken Farm."

"I confess, I dearly love a pretty little chicken," Harry said. "Nothing sweeter than a good layer."

"Well, say, then, whyn't you come with me, now," Farmer Cox said. "We can talk whilst we look around." He started toward the barn. "Folks 'round here say our chickens are the sweetest."

Sylvester-now-Harry fell in step with him. "That's music to my ears," he said. "Yes, sir. Music to an old chicken-lover's ears."

EPILOGUE

"Happy Birthday, Bunny." Teri offered him the gift-wrapped box.

"But it's not my birthday," Peter said, surprised.

Teri shrugged and grinned. "The way I see it," she said, "a birthday is your own personal holiday, isn't it? You can celebrate it anytime you want. Go ahead, open it."

She watched with bright, somewhat anxious eyes as he tugged at the pink bow, undid the ribbon and tore off the white paper. "Nice wrapping," he said.

She shrugged. "Lee did it for me," she said. "You know how lousy I am at that sort of thing."

The box inside was taped shut. He pried the tape loose with a fingernail and lifted the lid off the box. Inside was a layer of lavender tissue paper, neatly folded. He unfolded it, and stared, a puzzled expression on his face. He poked at the contents with one finger. Finally, he lifted them out of the box.

"They're panties," Teri said, growing more apprehensive. *Shit, what if she'd gotten it wrong? What if he was insulted?*

"Women's panties," he said, his face expressionless.

"Yes," she admitted nervously.

He read the teal-blue embroidery on the sheer pink silk. "*Mais l'amour viendra.*"

"It's French. It means love will come. That's what the saleslady told me, anyway."

"A little foreign tongue," he said.

"What?"

"Oh…nothing," he said, "Just something I remember hearing one time."

He lifted his eyes but still he did not look directly at her. He looked past her at the window, his face still blank. "Did Lee know what he was wrapping?" he asked after a moment.

"Absolutely not. The box was taped when he wrapped it. Well," she shrugged helplessly, "he might have guessed, I suppose. From the size and all. You know, woman's intuition. If he did, he didn't say. I would never have told him. Honest. This is just between the two of us."

The silence grew long. She began to feel like all kinds of a fool. It had seemed like such a good idea when she had seen them at Macy's, and a way to pique his interest. Now....

"Excuse me," he said, his face still offering no clue to how he was feeling. He took the box with him and went into the bedroom, closing the door after himself.

Double shit, she thought. She sat frozen in her chair, staring at the closed door. Was he pissed? Hurt? Embarrassed? *I should have had my head examined.* She felt like kicking herself.

The minutes stretched into what seemed hours. Her mouth was as dry as dust. She thought that she ought to say something to him, yell an apology through the door, or at least an explanation.

That was it, really, she ought to have talked to him about how she felt, not just have sprung something on him like this. No wonder he was in shock.

She was about to get out of her chair, go to the door, when it opened. She caught her breath. Peter was wearing the pink panties—and nothing else. And there was no question about the effect of them on his sexual state of mind. The way they were being stretched, she suspected that the sheer pink silk wasn't long for this world.

He paused in the doorway, smiling shyly, his erection jutting proudly forward. "What do you think? Are they my color?" he asked. "How do they look?"

All right, she thought deliriously. She reached down and pulled her tee shirt up and off.

"Good enough to eat," she said.